I0581566

kate mckinney

When to Hold On

Spiral North Books

For all the quiet people

The Driftless Area

In the American Upper Midwest, a unique subregion called the Driftless Area spans over 24,000 square miles. While there exist no formal boundaries, this area encompasses what we now call southwestern Wisconsin (a.k.a. the Western Upland or Ocooch Mountains), as well as the corners of southeastern Minnesota, northeastern Iowa, and northwestern Illinois. This land, also known as the Paleozoic Plateau, was formed between 538.8 and 251.9 million years ago. Its sedimentary strata are a combination of dolomite, limestone, and sandstone. The region's rugged terrain is due to having been avoided by glaciers for the last several million years. Glaciers are mile-high rivers of ice that crush and bulldoze everything in their paths. Glacial "drift" is the debris (sand, silt, gravel, and boulders) trapped and transported by glaciers and then left behind as they recede. This unglaciated land does not have such debris. Thus, early geologists named it "*drift*-less." Over millions of years, rivers and their tributaries cut deeply into the land, leaving behind steep, narrow valleys, high hills, bluffs, ridges, and rock outcrops. It is a rare landscape rich with biodiversity and unique microclimates, and has a high concentration of cold-water streams.

SUMMER
FALLS
TO
AUTUMN

GIRL MEETS GIRL

The only sound
in the public library's vestibule
comes from the pages I turn
as I sort through discarded magazines
until

a girl
crashes into the quiet
like a cold splash in the August heat.
      I try to step aside

meet turquoise
burnt sienna
the smell of cinnamon
green eyes that sink deep,
      like soft rain soaking parched soil.

My heart skips.   It's a moment
      or eons
before that girl moves around me,

swings the second door open,
walks through.

FRIENDLY INQUIRY

I keep my head down,
trying to pass by the circulation desk undetected,
but no luck.
        "Hey, Brynn. Making another collage?"

It's Maggie—my mom's coworker and friend,
someone I've known all my life,
not someone I want to talk to right now.

I nod, holding up the free magazine. Wait a beat.

        "How's your mom?"
It's an invitation to talk.
Mom would.
        She'd gloss over her medical tests
        but describe her favorite nurses,
        the blueberry pancakes,
        card games with Grandma.

But I
have more questions
than answers.

I leave it all unsaid.

4

IN THE FAR CORNER

That girl
with hair the color of burnt sienna
cocks her head to the side and smiles.
        "This seat taken?"

I lurch forward, gesture to the empty chair,
want to say, *All yours.*
              But too tongue-tied,
I duck my head,
hold my breath tightly to my chest,
glimpse her turquoise scarf,
green, paisley tights,
black boots,
the open page of my sketchbook.

In this corner of Wisconsin
where glaciers never flattened our land
heavy rains in springtime combine with snowmelt,
gush down steep slopes so hard
they roar.
A person can hardly think over the sound.
But that massive amount of water pounding rock
can't compare to the pounding within me.

The vein in my thumb pulses
as I grasp my pen and try to draw
something,
anything,
if only to move my hand across the page,
give me something to do.

        "You an artist?"
she asks, not a hint of sarcasm.
Rather, a slow-moving, summer rainstorm
rumbling closer, filled with electric spark.

I would give anything to know how to answer,
but my words become scattered
as though I've dropped and dumped out
one of my envelopes—
clippings of words and photographs
that I store away for who knows when,
waiting to be used for one project or another.

Before too long, I realize *she's* still waiting
for an answer.

THE PAINTER

"I like to paint,"
she offers

which is just enough
to transform my silence into a question:

"What do you like to paint?"

Thankfully, it gets her talking instead.

She tucks a frizzy curl behind one ear.
        "For me…it's more about the way
        I see whatever I'm painting. I try to
        get up close
        or pick an unusual angle. Try to see
        what others might miss.
        I use lots of color because
        even grass isn't just green. It's also
        yellow and brown, blue and purple,
        even pink."

LIKE THE CREEK'S CURRENT

Her words
tumble freely

The light in her eyes
carries me downstream

She is mysterious
magnetic
marvelous

NAMES

We leap and bound
from art to astronomy,
ancient Egyptians to electric vehicles,
exchanging so many thoughts
but never
our own names.

Names seem unimportant—

a name
could not encapsulate
all that she is,
all that I feel I am
as we connect the dots
of what feels like the whole universe.

LEAVING THE LIBRARY

We are two loose leaves
passing on the breeze, swirling
Will we meet again?

ON MY WAY HOME

I step into Monty's Mini Mart,
buy eggs, milk, and bread for French toast,
tired of frozen pizzas or tuna fish salad.

My mind circles,
like one of Mom's favorite records,
replaying my conversation with that girl.

Locking eyes with her pulled forth
a fragile, quivering
part of myself,
as if drawn from the mud,
naked and raw,
ready.

I want this feeling to last,
like the final note of a song
sustained.

HOLDING THINGS TOGETHER

At home
our Prairie-Craftsman offers a slanted smile—
sloped porch, squeaky step.

I put groceries away, grab duct tape,
return to the porch where yew shrubs
cast a shadow.

Ever since we moved into this house
Mom has said she'll cut down those shrubs,
replace them with a pocket prairie.
She wants color and variety—
native flowers and tall grasses that welcome
not only us
but also, birds and butterflies.

But Mom's been in and out of the hospital.
Daniel, my stepdad, runs between there and work.
Those yews
grow bigger and bigger.

I consider going to the shed,
hauling out the loppers myself,
hacking those shrubs to pieces.

But I don't.

Mom wants to do it,
and I'm going to let her.
Everyone says she's going to beat this thing.
The yews
can wait.

I focus on the toe of my shoe,
the cracked rubber,
and wrap the split with duct tape.

ALL NIGHT

You an artist?

That girl's unanswered question

hangs in the air

A line of poetry separated from its poem

Stitching come undone

A drawer left open

A hand tugging at my shirt

CAT GOT YOUR TONGUE?

That girl has all the words in the world
and lets them spill over like an overflowing cup.
Whereas I
clutch every word
like the scraps of letters and photos
I clip and stash.

Cat got your tongue?
Grandma used to say to me
before Mom told her
to knock it off.

But that girl is new in town.
She doesn't know people complain that I'm
too quiet.
Doesn't know to ask about Mom being sick.
She's going to be a junior like me.

If a girl like that
can talk to me once,
who knows what else might happen?

MY PLAN

Like the bending trees beside me
dipping their thirsty roots,
I dip my fingers into the cold creek,
dig into warm, silky mud,
while that girl's words sink in.
She drinks hot chocolate year-round
because even in summer
air conditioning makes her cold,
and she gets hers at Compass Café
where they add cinnamon
just like her nana used to do.
That is how I come up with my plan.
It's way out of my comfort zone,
because coffee shops are full of people.
But I want to know—if we talked again
could that raw part of myself become
something more?

HOPEFUL

Even from the bottom of Main Street,
I can see the logo on the side of the awning
over the café door.

Splashes of yellow and green color
the café's signature flower,
commonly known as
the compass plant.

I always liked that the flower got its name
for the reliable way the plant grows.

Its lobed leaves
orient themselves vertically,
pointing north and south,
turning their flat surfaces to face
east and west
maximizing carbon gain
and water efficiency
while avoiding getting scorched
by the sun's strongest rays.

For ages, humans have used these
natural compasses

to find their bearings

But who knows how long this plant
evolved and changed
until it found the best way
to thrive
within the stresses of its environment.

Compass plants stand tall, with multiple blossoms,
sticking their necks out
like hopeful, gangly teenagers.

Perhaps I look like one,
loping up this hill.

SUN RISES, SUN SETS

Each morning, my hope
rises with the sun,
riding on the back of best intentions.
Each evening, it falls
with the setting sun.
I walk toward the café,
aiming to talk with that girl.
Only, as soon as the door is within reach,
my feet carry me to the woods instead.
Today is the worst.
Through the window
I see her laughing with another girl.
This, on top of Mom's lab results,
sends me running
straight to the creek, to my rock.

THE TIME IT TAKES

I press my cheek
against this limestone slab, a stubborn jaw
out over the creek.

My chance with that girl seems gone
like yesterday's water.

I lay disappointment on top of fear.

I return to the same old unanswered questions,
wait
for the next plan
to be drawn up and played out
by Mom's medical team.

Curbing my impatience,
I deepen my breath, focus
on this rock beneath me, cool and textured.
Remember
that it took hundreds of millions of years
to become what it is today.
Layers and layers of seashells had to stack up
and sit through time
under great amounts of pressure.

Compared to this rock,
I know nothing
of what it means
to wait.

It will take the time it takes.
I must be as patient
as this rock.

BOOTS AND SHOES

Sitting next to Mom's hospital bed
I'm a rabbit in the bushes.
My ears twitch at every blip.
Machines attached to her body
monitor everything
from her heart rate
to oxygen level
to who knows what.

I thrust my legs forward,
wishing I could get up, walk
down the hall, push through the double doors,
with no more than a casual, "See you later!"
tossed over my shoulder, like I used to say
whenever I left her office at the library.

Mom notices the duct-tape
wrapped around the toe of my shoe.
Her voice maneuvers around her swollen tongue,
a raspy whisper.
     "Brynn, all that time in the woods,
      you need a good pair of boots."

My cheeks flush.

"Daniel will take you shopping…."

I push her concern away, tell her,
"They're fine."

My shoes are molded to my feet,
making it easy to slide down to the creek.
So what if the rubber is cracked, canvas torn?
I tuck my feet back underneath my chair,
paste a smile across my face.

I want her to know I will not
be letting go so quickly
just because something looks
tired and broken.

VISITING HOURS

Mom has always had a knack
for getting people talking—
even me.
But since she's been in the hospital,
there's a whole lot of silence between us.

I'm down to a trickle.

Anything I might want to say
feels like a bother.
Superstition
chokes any *what if?*

Better to wait. Not say anything out loud,
in case it tips the scales too far.

In the evening
> Grandma chit-chats,
> Grandpa tells stories,
> even Daniel has things to say.

My unspoken words
stack and compress.

I WANT TO TELL MOM

About the girl from the library.
About my wish
to get close to her,
see the shape of every freckle,
hear the whisper of every breath.

I want to confess
I lost my nerve.

I KNOW

Mom would be the first
to tell me:
Go talk to that girl.

My mom, the talker.

My mom, who always said,
> *Don't let the world tell you*
> *who you are*
> *or what you can or cannot do.*

Even with her skin translucent
and her eyes dark and sunken,
her expression still says,
> *I won't.*

GOSSIP

In our small town, Prairie Hill,
people can be kind

and cruel.

They can talk
but also whisper.

When Mom returned
to my grandparents' farm
with only one semester left of college,
she knew her secret wouldn't last long.

Instead of hiding her pregnancy,
her voice spread kindness
and acceptance.
She wiped counters and took orders
at the Dine-In,
volunteered at the library.

She overcame rumors
about who
my father was
or was not

by telling them
that
wasn't the interesting part of the story.

She'd point to her round belly
and laugh.
        "Now, *this* one
        is the story."

My mom finished her degree online
and went to Madison for Library Science.
By the time this small town
hired her as Library Director,
the whispers about

who

had long faded.

When *I* got to asking,
she said
I was all hers

and no amount of gossip
would ever change that.

28

TIME'S UP

Daniel's hand touches my shoulder.

We stand
each take a turn
saying just five words:

"Love you.
See you later."

I promise to say more
tomorrow.

MORNING

Somewhere between asleep and awake
I try to identify what that buzzing sound is.

I recall my grandparents driving me home
while Daniel stayed overnight at the hospital.
Grandma stayed with me,
even though I told her she didn't have to.
She told me to get some sleep.
It took me ages to finally drop off.

I blink at the time: 6:14.
Pull the blanket over my head
because isn't summer all about sleeping in?

Then it clicks: that buzzing
is my phone. I snap awake.

THE CALL

Daniel's voice comes heavy
like a rolling fog
      "Take a deep breath."
I can't.
Only hear
      "Get yourself ready.
      …your mom…   infection
            …Code Blue…
      …Hank is on his way to pick you up."
My insides rattle
      …hurry, hurry….
I meet Grandma at the door,
bang out of the house, then   wait
at the end of the driveway,
looking for the first sign of Grandpa's truck.

DESPERATE

"Why don't we take Mom's car?"
I point to the green hatchback
parked in the driveway.

Grandma shakes her head.
        "I don't know if it has enough gas.
        Don't worry.
        Your grandfather will be here
        any minute."

"We don't *have* a minute!"

And then the truck rounds the corner.
I run to meet him.

TOO SLOWLY

Shoulder to shoulder
the three of us
watch the road as we pass mile after mile
of countryside,
drive through construction
at the edge of Madison.

When we turn onto Monroe Street, I dial Daniel.
"We're almost there."

He says too slowly,
        "That's good.
                Tell Hank not to rush."

That makes no sense.

        "Brynn,"
His voice breaks,
        "I'm sorry
                ...she's gone."

PAVEMENT

A siren wails
     and from a long, dark corridor, I realize
the sound
comes from   me.
Grandpa swerves the truck,
                    stops.
     I pull the lever
          push the door open,
crawl out,
     barely catching my balance on the curb.
I run
       hard
         in the opposite direction.
     There is nowhere to go.
     Nothing but concrete and pavement.
       Boutique shops and restaurants.
Isolated   trees   at   regular   intervals.
I turn down a side street,
       house after house,
    gardens and trees
but it all belongs to other people.
There's no
     hillside prairie to run through,
       no woods to get lost in,

no rock to cling to.
I collapse.
Maybe I hear Grandma call my name,
but all that I'm certain of
are the tiny grooves in the cement
digging into my wet cheeks.

AWAY

Grandma finds me,
but I am barely there.
She holds me
somewhere in the city
but I don't feel her touch.
I'm too far
away.

ONLY SLEEPING

We're allowed in to see Mom.

The nurse tells us she's been cleaned up
and to take all the time we need.

There's a curtain to pull back,
the bed to walk around.

Her long, brown hair
drapes around her pale cheeks.

I know the truth.
She is dead.

But I try to tell myself
she is only sleeping.

NOT MOM

The box is small.
Wooden.
Daniel's calloused hands hold it up
like a fragile bird.
He looks at me with full-moon eyes,
his toes barely touching the living room carpet.
He says,
     "Here's Mom,"
but his eyes plead,
          May I come in?

I sit
knees to chin
in the orange armchair,
fingering tufts of stuffing
bulging from the torn tweed ends of the armrest.
It's what I used to do, curled up next to Mom,
listening to her stories,
her heartbeat mixing with the rhythm of her voice.

My stepdad is a kind man.
Well-meaning.
But he's wrong.

The box was handcrafted
by my mother's best friend from high school,
an artist who turns reclaimed wood
into fine art.
My mother would've loved it.

But that is not Mom.

According to her wishes,
Daniel told the funeral director
cremation.
I sat next to him, numb.
Haunted by the process,
what it looked like,
until my mind skipped to the end—
dust, ash.

Not Mom.

Now, I keep expecting her
to walk around the corner,
tell me, "One more thing…."
Or I hear the room crack open,
in my mind's ear, from her laugh.
Her laugh that filled the house
all the way to the rafters.

Until I realize it's still
quiet.

Not Mom.

MEMORIAL SERVICE

Grandma finds me next to the snack table.
Only, I'm not eating.
        "Everyone is looking for you,"
she scolds,
then ushers me back to the receiving line.

If only
everyone would stop talking,
maybe I could catch a breath
in this stuffy room, filled shoulder-to-shoulder.

If only
people would stop saying,
        "Your mom
            was such a wonderful person."
Like I don't already know.

Stop saying,
        "Your mother
            is in a better place now."

Better
would be her walking in the woods with me
and all these people at home.

FORMER FRIENDS

Isobel, my mom's best friend,
the artist who made the wooden box,
enters like a wave.

Isobel doesn't roll out polite condolences.
Nearly a head taller than me,
she reaches out, pulls me in,
layers of flowing fabric, soft around my face.
Never one to push or prod,
she could always be counted on
to take me exactly as I am.

In her embrace, I wonder for one second
if I could let myself fall to pieces.

At one time, she'd felt like a second mother.
But Isobel's daughter, Nina—
with all her sharp edges—
trails behind her, too close.

Nina and I grew up together—
wherever she went,
I followed

until
the summer after eighth grade
when Nina
got in with the popular crowd
and she told me
in no uncertain terms
not
to come along.

ESCAPE

All those months that my mom was sick,
Nina never offered a kind word.

Acted as though she didn't know. Of course,
she did.

I have nothing to say to her
and don't want to hear what she might say now.

Faking a coughing attack, I excuse myself,
escape to the bathroom.

AFTERWARDS

My grandparents, Daniel, and I sit
in our living room, tired and drained.
I won't look at the box of Mom's ashes
resting on the coffee table.
My mind is chaotic
with the memory of the day's voices
but this quiet
feels like crashing cymbals.

THEY DON'T KNOW

They all look at me
with eyes that seem to say
  I know what it's like.

Only they don't.
They can't.
No one can.

MISTAKE

Daniel clears his throat.
       "Brynn, your mother wanted you
       to choose the place to bury…or scatter
       …her ashes."
His voice is gentle, yet his words slam me.

No.
I must've misheard. This cannot
be happening. My eyes
don't blink,   water on their own accord.
Mom would never
ask me to do something like that.
She would never
because she was going to get better.

Grandma sits up straight.
       "What about the family plot?"

The tiny cemetery where all our ancestors
have been buried since settling in Wisconsin.

Daniel shrugs.
       "It's in her will and testament.
       Brynn is to decide."

No. She would never.

Grandpa tries to calm Grandma
by putting an arm around her shoulders—
the same action he's done hundreds of times
whenever she and my mom argued.

No one else seems to notice
the obvious mistake—
that this conversation cannot be real
because Mom
was going to *get better*.

Grandma's lips tighten into a firm line.
No one says anything more.
But like all those other
hundreds of times,
I can tell,
this won't be the last I'll hear of this.

DAILY ROUTINE

Daniel stays out of my way,
and I stay out of his.
The more we don't talk,
the more we can't.

FRIENDS

The restored prairie and oak savanna
are where I meet my only circle of friends—
black-eyed Susan,
compass plant,
cup plant,
pale purple coneflower.
These are the familiar faces I count on.
Native bur oaks
welcome me with their out-stretched branches.
It's the closest I get to not feeling so alone.

PERSEIDS

Hundreds of meteors plunge to Earth,
streak across night sky,
offering a plethora of wish-making
on the backs of shooting stars.

I was eight years old the first time
Mom and I walked through the restored prairie
in mid-August to watch the meteor shower.
I whined
about not being on my grandparents' farm.
Mom and I had just moved
into our own apartment in town.
Just the two of us.
Mom said it was time
for her to stand on her own two feet.
I was wishing we could move back to the farm,
but it was that night she explained
I was never too far from our old home.
The prairie led to woods,
which led to the boundary of the farm.
I would always be connected
through the roots of plants.
      "And the same sky,"
she pointed.

"…is over all our heads."
We returned to the prairie every year
to watch the sky and make wishes.

But what is the use now?
No matter how many shooting stars I see,
my wish for Mom back
can never be granted.

LABOR DAY, THE FARM

I can't help it—
as soon as Daniel's truck stops,
I dart out, throw, "See you later,"
over my shoulder,
run to the back woods.
I haven't taken a deep breath in a week.
But here, among tall trees, I'm my old self again.
Free.
Where Mom
taught me to dip my toes
into cold spring water,
build secret hideaways
out of old fallen tree branches,
lay down on a thick bed of white pine needles.
Here, I can breathe.

COMING BACK

Mud on my shoes
soft breeze off the pond
song of a whip-poor-will

Could be last year for all I know.
                    Not a care in the world.

Porch light is switched on.
Must be later than it feels.

OUT OF NOWHERE

Grandma's voice comes sharp.

     "We can't keep waiting!"

I freeze. Am I that late?

Is she calling me to dinner through the window?

Guess it is getting dark.

Her voice goes on, rises and falls:

     "…too young…won't even talk…"

Skin tingles. She's not calling me.

She's talking *about* me.

I creep closer along deep purple shadows,

hear Daniel.

     "It's up to Brynn. Lori wanted—"

but I stop listening.

Pound my feet loud on the porch steps,

let the screen door slam.

DINNER TO GO

Grandma stands.
Nearly knocks down her kitchen chair.
"About time."
Food sits out, but plates are scraped clean.
"Is it too much to ask
that you eat dinner with us?"
I steal a glance at Grandpa chewing his lip,
rubbing his arthritic knee.
Daniel rises.
"Sadie, Hank,
thank you for dinner.
It's time for us to go."
As if on cue, my stomach growls. Wish it hadn't.
Grandma shoots Daniel a look as if to say, *See?*
Daniel rubs the back of his neck.
I offer to eat at home—
the wrong thing to say, of course.
Grandma turns to the cupboard.
Gets out an empty yogurt container.
Returns to the table, starts scooping food.
"Here,"
she thrusts the container into my hands,
"at least eat something homecooked.
You're all skin and bones."

THE TRUTH

Daniel's truck leaves a wake of dust
down the gravel driveway.
Gripping the sides of the yogurt container,
I wonder how to cut through
all that hasn't been said.   I blurt—
"It's not like Mom told me   where
she wanted to be buried."

Daniel turns onto the county highway.
We pass row after row of towering corn.
My words dangle in the silent cab.

Threshing time is coming.
I imagine the fields after harvest
when whirling winds
will pick up loose dried husks
like paper birds taking flight.

Out of the quiet comes Daniel's voice,
     "We're all   grieving,"
as if telling himself,
     "...and grief muddles everything.
     You'll know what to do
     when the time is right."

THE NIGHTMARE

An open window
White lace curtains
Cherry blossoms
A lazy breeze

Mom sits up in bed,
smiles

Doctors whisper from a dark hallway.
Mom looks between here
                        and death

Eye-piercing brightness quickly dissolves the room

            I scream

Mom doesn't hear
            No one comes

The brightness expands until
            even she is gone.   There is only my scream
                                of silence

I am   nothing, nowhere

58

LIFE MARCHES ON

First day of school
and off I walk
down dappled streets,
kids wearing new backpacks.

CHAOS

The high school is utter chaos,
bodies crammed together
like salmon swimming upstream.
It's a collage of sound—
clippings of phrases about summer vacations,
and yet no one here cuts through the noise
to get to me to shoot the breeze.

The school counselor
        wears her "Welcome Back!" smile,
        but the memory of how hard she tried
to get me talking last spring
makes it hard to breathe
because talking about my feelings
is the last thing I need.

I keep my head down.   Hope to dodge
        all eyes.
Try to blend with the cement-blocked walls.
Get lost in the crowd.

BUT BEFORE FIRST BELL

Miss Popular, otherwise known as
Queen of Gossip
slides up next to my locker,
says in her syrupy voice,
        "Brynn, I *heard* about your mom—
        I can't imagine
        what you're going through."

There's a pause
        she expects me to fill.

I don't
and won't.

Closing my locker door,
I pretend to take her offer of sympathy as genuine
even though it's clearly a dig for information.

I say, "Thank you,"
then walk away.

FINDING MY PLACE

Holding tight to my schedule
I zigzag through the crowd
to room 201.
My first class:
Ecology.

I lock my eyes
onto the white floor tiles,
skirt around the doorframe

scan the first row of chairs
nearest the door

take the empty seat
in the back corner.

THAT GIRL

Kitty-corner, across the room,
a single backward glance
from that girl
holds mine
a moment too long,
not long enough.
I spend the rest of the hour
adding up glimpses —
the tilt of her chin,
sunlight through a maze of sienna curls,
her black boots tapping against the tile floor.

DESTINY

Of all the elective courses to choose
why did she pick Ecology?
I'll never admit
to such foolish thinking out loud,
but I wonder
if it's Destiny.

ROLL CALL

Every morning for two weeks,
when Mr. Lewis calls out,
    "Brynn Bailey?"

I respond
like the tree frog's trill in spring.
Cricket's chirping at night.

I anticipate that girl's name:
    "Zoe McClain?"

Wait for her reply.
A sound that croons.

Smiles flash across the room
like fireflies searching for a mate.
Lights flashing,
    Here I am. Come closer.

TURN THE LOCK

When I get home
Grandma's waiting on the porch swing.
Crisscrossed ankles and a plump-cheeked smile
give the pretense of Miss Mild Manners,
but I sense her ready to pounce.
Sure enough, she does.
      "I'd like to make arrangements…"
Burial arrangements, her pause implies.
      "…before the ground gets too hard."

I turn the key in the lock, open the door.
She follows me inside.
      "Have you given more thought
      to your decision?"
I drop my bag in the hallway, go to the fridge.
Don't answer.
      "Brynn, it's not good
      for any of us to let this go on
      indefinitely."
I slam the fridge door, snap around.
"All you want
is to be done with it! Done with her!"
She steps back.
      "No.

I want a place
for my daughter to be.
A place
for all of us to go to.
Somewhere for her to rest.
Is that so wrong?"

A fire rages through my body. "She won't be
resting! *To rest* means you can wake up—"

But I've come too close. Said too much.
A cold wave
rises, chokes the flame,
reducing me
to a puff of smoke.

I push past her, run upstairs,
slam my bedroom door, turn the lock.
Don't come down until long after
I hear her leave.

WALKING TO THE CREEK

My feet fall into rhythm
walking north through town,
toward the creek.

Grandma's words mix
with the crisp change in the air,
autumn rounding the corner.
> *...it's not good*
> *for any of us to let this go on*
> *indefinitely.*

I tuck my hands into my long sweater sleeves
wondering how to explain that, right now,
all I can do is hold on. All I can decide
is to take a single breath, put one foot
in front of the other.

QUAKING ASPENS

I remember Mom walking beside me
across town
past this same stand of quaking aspen,
pointing to golden-tipped leaves
fluttering against the clear September sky.
     Look at that gold! That blue!
It was a game, a way of life for us.

Who else takes time to look?

Zoe flashes to mind.

The sound of shaking leaves
brings Mom's voice.
     Talk to her.

BEFORE FIRST BELL

I listen
to the chatter
inside and outside myself.
Let it all
dissipate
disintegrate
dissolve
before becoming one sleek stream of motion—
chasing destiny,
all the while wondering at the paradox—
why chase
something inevitable?
If it is destiny, why
hunt it down?

ASKING

All at once I am across the room
standing before Zoe.
The corner of her mouth quivers,
then flips into a smile.
My voice ripples out,
asking if she wants to meet me
at Compass Café,
and she says,

        "Sure, why not?

        How about Saturday?"
Although I'm sure I'm blushing,
I'm also nodding,
and I'm lucky to remember just in time
to ask, "Three o'clock?"
She agrees.

        "See you then."
Adrenaline gets me back to my seat,
but I have no idea
what
Mr. Lewis talks about
for the rest of the hour,
because I can only think:
I did it.

AT THE CAFÉ

I wait

and wait

and as the hands of the clock on the wall
walk their way around the block
reality settles onto my shoulders:

Zoe is not coming.

Tables have filled
and emptied.
I push pen over paper,
round and round,
filling white space with deep,
dark circles.
My mind fills in reasons why.

At last, my pen is still.

Zoe wants nothing to do with me.

WHAT'S IN A NAME?

No longer waiting, I push through the café door,
cool air flooding my lungs.
I get into stride, head for the creek.

Most days, roll call
is the only chance
to hear my name spoken aloud.

But before I reach the end of the block,
        "Brynn!"
cuts through the silence
like the glow of afternoon sunlight
cutting low through tree branches.

The sound of her saying it
catches my breath,
turns my feet.

STILL

I invite Zoe to walk with me
through restored prairie,
between oak and hickory,
down to the creek,
right to my usual limestone rock.
Checking upstream, then down, she asks,
    "You come here often?"
I nod, then hand her a small stone.
She turns it around in her fingers,
looks at it closely, then slips it into her pocket.
Her body fidgets
as though words can't wait to escape.
I dig my heels into the quiet and sit
still.
I can't make her listen,
but I do
carve out space.

TOUCH

Zoe's fingertips playfully brush my arm
quick as a flash
just as quick as her words come and go,
but then her fingers pause
the way a dragonfly hovers over water,
its wings vibrating so fast, they buzz.
But maybe that's just me because my whole body
is tingling with warmth.
And although her lips have stopped moving
and a wisp
of quiet
sits between us,
this is something loud and wonderful.

ECOLOGY PROJECT

Mr. Lewis explains the semester's major project,
worth a third of our grade,
then lets us loose to choose partners.
Zoe glides down the aisle,
sits in the empty seat next to mine,
asks with no doubt in her voice,
      "You want to be partners?"
I cock one eyebrow and tease, "I don't know.
What do you have in mind?"
She laughs.
      "No idea. You?"
I laugh too. "None whatsoever."
Like two monkeys, we grin.

WALKING OUT TOGETHER

Zoe says,
> "Let's go to the library after school.
> We can figure out our project.
> Meet at my locker?"

I haven't been back to the library since before
Mom died.
They've already hired a new director. But no one
can replace Mom.

If I say anything to Zoe, the sparkle in her eyes
might dim. This moment, lost. Anyway, I can't
talk about it.

Won't.

Maggie, the assistant librarian,
will ask how I'm *doing*. Zoe will know
something's up.

I think fast.
"How about we brainstorm at the creek,
then go to the *school* library
during class tomorrow.

It's too nice to stay cooped up.
Anyway, my stepdad runs Prairie Hill Nursery.
He has plenty of books we can borrow."

She agrees and doesn't seem to notice
I've sidestepped the truth.
I release a breath as she walks away,
but right on the heels of my relief
comes nagging guilt.

RETURNING TO THE CREEK

I lead Zoe down the path
but don't say much
until

I start pointing out plants
native
invasive

plants that tell a story of the land's history

How, prior to colonization,
native people managed the land with fire
for thousands of years,
regenerating prairie and bur oak savannah
until

European settlers came,
believing and repeating a myth—
that this land was "pristine wilderness,"
"untouched by humans,"
that it needed to be cut down or plowed up,
that fire was to be feared, suppressed

Thus, soil lost nutrients year after year,

washing down steep slopes,
no longer kept in check by deep prairie roots,
strong oaks

The corners of land untouched, unburned,
became crowded
by quick growing maples,
buckthorn, and honeysuckle.
Oak savanna gave way
to woodland without mature understories

Food seeds and medicinal herbs,
brought from the old country,
further changed the face of the land,
for garlic mustard loves disturbed soil,
but no native animal
loves eating it.

At the sound of the creek
I mention the cold-water trout at risk
due to pollution
and warming waters because of climate change,
then realize I've been rambling nonstop
about the one thing
I can: the Driftless Area.

IT'S DECIDED

"Of course!" I say, shaking my head, laughing,
hardly believing it took me this long.
"Let's
do our presentation on the Driftless Area."

I offer my hand to help her navigate
        the slope to the creek.
She focuses on her footing, but says,
        "I didn't even think
        about our *own* ecosystem.
        I figured we had to do something like
        the Amazon rainforests."

Our hands let go when we reach the rock.
She finds her side, I, mine.

"Well, if we're talking endangered ecosystems,
the Midwest is, sadly, a great place to start."
Her eyebrows raise in question. I continue,
"Less than a *tenth* of a percent
of the region's native prairie and oak savanna
that thrived
before colonization
still exists.

Yet, prairies are chock-full of biodiversity.
They build and retain healthy soil,
and sequester carbon-dioxide from the air.
They're invaluable to the planet.
Pockets of the Driftless Area
even host rare species
found during glacial periods 10,000 years ago."

Zoe's eyes go wide.
        "Really?"
My body tingles.
"Amazing, right?

"This region is unique to the world,
but most people know nothing about it.
And the longer people don't know
and understand,
the more change for the worse.
Our country's already big mono-culture farms
keep expanding,
digging up more land for corn and soybeans,
and urban sprawl eats away the land that's left,
which all leads to soil erosion and compaction.
Nutrients are washed away,
our streams suffer from runoff,
and *we* suffer because of more flooding."

I could go on, get into my latest reading
about agroforestry
permaculture
as well as Daniel's work with prairie restoration,
        but I change direction,
remembering something Zoe said
the first day we met.

I lean forward,
"If we do our project on our *local*
ecosystem,
we won't have to just read articles online,
we'll be able to get an *up-close* look."

I wait a beat,
hope she'll remember what she said about art.
Hope she'll realize
I listened.

She laughs.
        "Perfect!"

SEE

Zoe leans back on her elbows.
      "I keep telling my mom that *we*
      need to do more.
      I mean, she knows about the issues.
      Melting polar icecaps, pollution,
      dwindling forests. All that. But
      she sees it as somebody else's problem,
      and doesn't really get why I took Ecology
      other than it's an elective that'll look good
      on my transcripts."

It's hard for me to imagine
because, lately, plants and ecology
are all Daniel and I *can*
talk about.
But I say

"I think a lot of people still don't want
to believe it matters.
Or they're stuck in old ways of thinking.
Some farmers outright dismiss
the changes they witness firsthand.
Flooding. Droughts. Whole crops lost.
They rely on the hope that it'll be better

next year."

She nods.
    "Which is exactly why
    we need to look closely—
    really see."

PEOPLE

Zoe tilts her head back. I follow her gaze, up
through the trees to blue sky.
        "Do you think humans
        really have a place in nature?"

This girl, my insides sing.   *This girl*
        asks the big questions.
        I love it.

"I do."

Zoe stretches her legs out in front of her,
wiggles her toes,
frowns.
        "Sometimes
        I think we've messed up so much
        maybe
        we should just step aside."

I shake my head.   "We *are*
part of nature.   Our mistake
is that we ever thought we weren't.

"We've destroyed

not because we're actually separate
or simply cruel,
        but because we forgot.
        We thought
we were different,

"that all of nature was for humans to use.
When in reality,
we are each one piece
of a larger whole.
One strand in a huge web."

Zoe's brow furrows.
        "But how do we fix
        the damage we've done?"

"That's just it," I sit up straighter,
"That word *fix*
keeps us separate still—it's not only about us.

"Yes, we need to take responsibility,
we need to work to make things better,
but, to do that,
we need to pay attention—we need to connect
to the whole web.
Realize

we *all* play a part in healing—we need to *all*
be part of the solution.
We need to *listen*.

"We depend on each other—
animals, plants, birds, insects, fungi,
rocks, water....

"Earth is a huge, complex system
with so many smaller systems that all relate.
It's about cultivating those relationships.
We need to see those connections,
find a balance."

I catch my breath.

Zoe's eyes shine back at me. She teases,
        "I didn't know you had so much to say."
I bite my lip

notice her beautiful, lopsided grin,
sparkling eyes,
then I laugh.
"Neither did I."

GOING BACK

Taking a different trail
we round a certain bend,
find an old bur oak.
Thick, corky bark peeled off.
Branch after branch

fallen.

This tree once stretched
burly limbs over swaying prairie.
Ready and willing to stand up
to wind and fire.

Now it's a skeleton in the woods.

THROUGH HER EYES

Zoe cranes her neck, gazing up at the tree.
      "It's like a sculpture.
      Those angles,
      the light and shadows."

She lifts a fallen piece, cradles it in her arms,
her fingers brushing
over its smooth, weathered curves.
      "It's too beautiful to leave behind."

I could say it's not wasted, there on the ground.
It's a host for all kinds of new life—
bacteria, fungi, critters scrounging for shelter.
But I resonate with the feeling behind her words.
I remember my duct-taped shoes.
Mom.

An idea begins to form.
Maybe even a clue, or riddle,
if only I can puzzle it out.

Zoe takes one side, and I, the other.
We carry that piece together
all the way home.

WEIRD

On my front porch
we shake out our muscles,
tired from carrying the piece of wood
all that way.

Zoe wonders aloud if it was weird
to take it home.
      "That's me—pretty weird."
She says it like a warning, then laughs.

I laugh too. Shake my head.
"Best idea ever."

Before I can invite Zoe inside, her phone rings.
Zoe has to get to her mom's office
ASAP.

I watch Zoe walk away
still listening to her mom over the phone.

JUNK MAIL AND BILLS

Not yet wanting to accept
the end of our time together,
I walk to the mailbox
to get a few more breaths of fresh air
and maybe one last glimpse
of Zoe at the end of our street.

Then she's out of sight, and all that's left
is a pile of junk mail and bills.

Inside, I throw the stack on the counter
next to the piles that Daniel set down
yesterday and the day before.

I return to the porch, hands on my hips,
considering the piece of wood, wondering
what it might become,
knowing that sometimes just asking the question
leads to something.

I bring it to my room
for safekeeping.

FRIDAY AFTERNOON

Beside my locker, Zoe murmurs my name—
water polishing stone.
>	"Told my mom I had a lot of homework,
>	with our project and all.
>	Said I was meeting you at Compass Café
>	tonight.
>	You in?"
Her eyes glint with mischief.
Nothing about her invitation
indicates we'll be getting much work done.
It makes me smile.
"Seven?" I propose.

DÉJÀ VU

Night steeps.

In front of the café,
blue reflections of the neon "OPEN" sign
dance across ripples in a black puddle.

Cool air sweeps around me.

I wiggle my toes, wonder—
will it be the same as last time?
Will Zoe make me wait?

I watch through the window.

Girls and guys flirt over schoolwork.
A woman at a laptop bites into a scone.
Zoe sits in the far corner, nose in a book.

As I step across the threshold
bells on the door ring louder
than my doubt.

MOMS

Zoe warms her hands around her steaming mug.
  "Sorry, but can I rant a minute?"

I'm curious and glad
for the excuse to just listen, instead of talk.
"Of course."

  "It's my mom.
  Today, instead of congratulating me
  on my near perfect score on my math test,
  she grilled me at length about the *one*
  I got wrong.
  If I eat a muffin in her car, she yells at me
  for getting crumbs
  on her precious car seats.
  It's like everything I do
  she has to correct.
  Is your mom like that?"

Hot liquid scalds my throat
as I swallow too quickly.

There's an empty beat
where I know I should tell Zoe:

My mom died this summer.

It plays out in my mind—
that look of pity.
Questions.
Concern.

It becomes
more about the other person
imagining my pain,
trying to find the right words
to comfort me.
Words that almost always
come out wrong.
Or they poke around
like I'm something to dissect.

I do *not* want to go there.

SO, I FAKE IT

I try a smile.
Try to match Zoe's tone.
Say something I might've said
back before Mom got sick.
"Yeah," I force a laugh.
"It's always *one more thing*, right?"

My throat catches. I feel sick to my stomach,
because now I'd trade a *million* more things
to have Mom back.

Zoe doesn't notice me look down,
blink away tears.
     "Exactly!
     I'm already taking AP classes.
     Now she wants me to do an internship
     next summer.
     She's a realtor, and her new boss
     wants a public relations assistant, only
     he's too cheap
     to hire someone,
     so he's made this out to be like some
     community outreach program."
Zoe rolls her eyes.

"She claims it's going to be
a chance of a lifetime.
Put my artistic eye to good use."
She shakes her head.
"I do not
want to spend all summer
at a computer
making boring flyers
about houses for sale.
That's *her* life. Not mine."

I lean forward.
"What do you want?"

It's as if the wind changes direction.
The golden glints in her eyes light up.
Her smile stretches.
"I wish I could take an art class
or paint a mural for a nonprofit, or
just paint and paint all day—
really dig into art somehow."
Her body sags.
"Mom says I have to be practical.
Use the summer to make some money,
save for college. And I get it, but
she won't listen when I try to tell her

I'm not into
her plan."

I nod but don't know what else to say,
so I just sit.
Wait.

"Anyway…."
She blushes, then shakes her head
as if trying to shake away her confession,
"Sorry for nattering on."

I shrug.
"You can tell me anything."

A slow glow seems to wash over her face.
"I've never known
someone that really listened
the way you do."

It's the nicest thing anyone's ever said
about me being so quiet.
It gives me an idea
and the courage to ask

"Want to get out of here?"

THE QUIET

I lead Zoe to the wooden retaining wall
that overlooks the restored prairie.
I take her hand
guide her through the dim moonlight
until we're sitting on the ledge.
She is not too quick to let go
and tingles race through me
even after we do.

I imagine kissing her.

"When things get to be…"
I bite my lip, "…too much,
but it's too dark to go down to the creek,
I come here. It helps…
to just listen."

Hardly a breath goes by before she says,
          "I love the sound of crickets."

Perhaps it's because we're in the open air
or because listening is what I do
but, somehow, I realize that maybe
her quick flying words

don't come from knowing just what to say
but rather, from being nervous.
I relax.

"Me too.
Do you hear that deeper tone?"
I hold my body still. So does she.
"Those are tree frogs."

She leans against me,
her whisper right beside my ear,
        "There must be tons."

I wonder if she feels our arms and thighs
touching
the way I do—
every cell in my body
wide awake.

From the valley
comes the crown jewel—
a low quiver:
        Hoo, Hoo, Hoo, Hoooo.
I hear the smile in her voice when she whispers,
        "An owl!"
I agree so quietly, it's almost a sigh.

Our ears strain to hear another call
and when it comes
we want more.

PIE FOR BREAKFAST

The sound of clinking dishes
wakes me at quarter to nine.
It's strange
because Daniel always leaves by 7:30.

I step gingerly down the stairs, to the kitchen,
wondering what kind of robber or ax murderer
stops to wash dishes?

Grandma is at the sink, wearing Mom's old apron,
washing the stack of three-day-old dirty dishes.
There's also a fresh-baked pie on the table.
Apple.
My favorite.

There's no mention of our last exchange.
Just a sunny greeting and an offer of pie.
She cuts a slice, winks, and says,
     "I won't tell, if you don't."
Apparently pie for breakfast is okay today.
I don't argue.

She sits across from me, chattering away,
while I chew.

Then she glances into the living room
and her voice trails off.
Every hair on my body stands on end.
        Mom's ashes.
This is why Grandma washed our dishes.
Why I'm eating pie for breakfast.
        "It's time we really talk
        about what to do."

I have only two bites left,
but I can't seem to swallow. I check the clock,
look down at my pajamas.
"Actually, I've got to go."
I bring my dirty plate to the sink.

        "Off to the creek?"

She knows me so well. But I tell her, "No.
School project."
Glad it's true.
I thumb toward the door. "I'm getting picked up.
Daniel's workshop."
I say it like she should already know.

"Thanks." I point to the pie and clean dishes,
then I dash upstairs.

104

PRAIRIE QUEST

Maybe Zoe had too much caffeine for breakfast
because when I open the front door,
her voice booms with drama:
>"We are the Knights
>of the Remnant Prairie!
>Do you, Sir Brynn,
>accept the challenge of our Quest?"
I can almost see the Sword of Courage
in her outthrust arm.
Her voice drips with melodrama.
>"We seek the seeds
>to change the course of history."
I bust out laughing.
She makes Daniel's seed-collecting workshop
sound way more interesting than it will be.
She stays in character.
>"A treacherous journey
>to save what's been lost
>to monocrops
>endless development
>and those filthy, invading shrubs!"
"*Someone's* taking her research seriously," I tease.
She breaks into a fit of giggles,   then

all within a string of seconds,
she's hugging me,
I start to sweat,
my cheeks burn,
and I wonder if it's a *friend* hug
            or an *I-want-to-be-your-girlfriend* hug.
I remember Grandma, still in our kitchen,
and I note Zoe's mom waiting in the SUV
parked in our driveway.
My heart pounds so loudly,
I'm sure they can all hear.
            "Let's go!"
Zoe says with a huge grin, already moving away,
and as I follow her through the cool morning air,
I realize I haven't laughed that hard
in a long, long time.

CHILL

As we slide into the backseat, Zoe's mom smiles
and introduces herself as Kim,
but as she drives down the street, I catch
her looking in the rearview mirror at me.
She seems to be calculating.

     "Zoe hasn't said much about today.

     What's the plan?"
Her voice has a slight edge, as though maybe
Zoe and she already talked, but Zoe's answers
were not satisfactory.
Before I can respond, Zoe leans forward.

     "Mom, I *told* you—

     we're just taking photos

     and collecting seeds."
Kim glances between my reflection and the road.

     "Your father owns Prairie Hill Nursery?"
The word *father* trips something inside of me.
My voice comes out small: "Yes,
my stepdad, Daniel."

     "I see."
She hands me a pen and notepad.

     "Please write down Daniel's contact info."
Zoe rolls her eyes,
then looks out the window for the rest of the ride.

NOT FAIR

We're heading to the front door
when Kim calls out.
      "You're sure
      Daniel won't mind
      dropping off Zoe?"

I turn.
Kim is leaning out her open window.
A ripple of compassion runs through me.
She seems so anxious.
I don't see why. I tell her, "No problem!"

Zoe groans.
      "Mom, we're going to be late!"
Her mother nods.
      "Call if you have any trouble."

Once inside, Zoe grumbles,
      "My mom is so anal."

Even though I know
she and her mom don't see eye-to-eye,
something about her annoyance
feels like a kick in my side.

Anger, like acid,
threatens to burn a hole through me.
I clench my jaw
to keep from exploding,
At least you have
a mom.

I stay quiet because I know
I'm not being fair—I haven't told
Zoe yet, and now
is not the time.

SHIFT

I already know Daniel's presentation
inside and out.

Instead of taking notes
I let the gentle cadence of his voice
settle around me, ease my tension.

Zoe's fingers grip her pencil.
Her brow furrows as she listens.

Later, walking through prairie as we collect seeds,
I lose track
of how many times she reaches in front of me
and I reach in front of her.
We take any excuse to touch.

We are two knights on a quest.
Two girls flirting.

AUTUMN FADES TO WINTER

INSIDE OUT

Laughing out loud, Zoe and I
run up the porch steps,
out of the wind and up into my room
until Zoe sees my collage over my bed
and stops cold.
      "Whoa."

Countless nature photos
overlap and words stick out, here and there,
over a four-foot by four-foot piece of cardboard.

She crawls up onto my bed to take a closer look
as I shift from one foot to the other,
like it isn't even my own room.

She whispers,
      "This is incredible."

I don't admit
that I made it to keep myself busy.
Don't admit
it filled in where my own words failed.
It was my silent prayer for *survival.*

I say, "That's how I got the idea
to use collage for our project—except…"
I step closer to the chunk of bur oak.
"…this one will be three-dimensional."

I'm eager to get started,
but Zoe is still looking
at my dresser top, windowsills,
edges of bookshelves, all cluttered with
acorns
sticks
leaves
rocks.

     "Guess I'm not so weird after all,"
she points to the bur oak wood,
     "…bringing that all the way here?"

I laugh at the memory and shake my head,
but raise one eyebrow and tease,
"Well…

     maybe weird like me?"
She laughs.
     "Absolutely."

OLD PHOTO

Zoe points to a tiny frame
tucked between the leaves of a draping
philodendron.
          "Is this you and your mom?"

I'm six years old in the photo.
Sledding behind my grandparents' farmhouse,
Mom's arms tight around me. Our screams
still ringing in my memory.

At the bottom of the hill, we tumbled.
I did a face plant in the snow. My cheeks burned
from the cold, but I came up laughing.
So did Mom.

Such a brief moment.

"Yes," I admit.

"YOU LOOK JUST LIKE HER"

Zoe says
what everyone else used to say.
      "All except for your hair, of course."

It's true. Mom and I
had the same
      willowy frame
      narrow cheekbones
      velvety brown eyes
      dark hair
But she wore hers long
down her back.
My haircuts have always been short.

Sometimes I wonder
if I grew my hair out
would it be like seeing Mom in the mirror?

CROSSROADS

I stand again at a crossroads.
I could tell Zoe right now:

My mom died.

Three little words.

Maybe I could even tell her about the ashes.
How Grandma keeps pushing.

I could spill it all.
Just get it out of the way.

But I've waited this long.
My insides burn, trying to decide.

TURNTABLE

Zoe laughs when she sees the record player.
      "Wow, I've only seen these in movies!"

Panic turns to disappointment,
spins round to guilt, the moment lost.

I take a breath,
point to the small collection. "Pick one."

Her face hovers close to mine
as I show her how to set the needle.
We watch the record spin
and listen to the opening notes—
a full orchestra and a rich, warm voice
echoing the question hanging between us:
sooner or later, we'll kiss, right?
This moment feels frozen, yet time keeps turning,
and as she steps away, my joy
of being right here with her inside the music
fades to *piano* as my mind turns back
to the question that blares like a trumpet—

when and how will I ever
tell Zoe about Mom?

COMING TOGETHER

Zoe tries to smear more glue over the clippings.
        "These had better start sticking.

Photos
of prairie grasses and forbs
in bloom and drying
scatter around us on the wooden floor.
We've cut pictures
from the digital prints taken on our Quest
and from old seed catalogues from Daniel.

Similar to my collage over my bed
we use a technique called decoupage,
overlapping and gluing cut-outs
around the smooth-worn surface
of the old, oak log we carried home.

        "Can't believe this is worth a third
        of our grade."
Zoe shakes her head.
        "Mom already thinks we're ridiculous
        for doing an art project
        instead of a written report."

It was Zoe's idea to use the log.
Mine, to do decoupage.

"It'll work. Here,"
I hold down the photo
while she smears more glue.
"Besides,
Mr. Lewis said it was fine."

She winks,
         "We're putting our art skills *to good use*."

I laugh. "Better than house flyers, right?"

         "No kidding!"

HUNGER FORCES US DOWNSTAIRS

Zoe butters bread
I lay down cheese
"Two slices?" I ask, reaching for more.

      "Definitely."

I top off the grilled-cheese sandwiches.
She stirs tomato soup.

Without Daniel home, I make the mental leap,
imagine this as our own home. That we're a
real couple.

Her elbow nudges my side.
      "Earth to Brynn."

I snap to, then blush when I smell burning butter.
I quickly flip the sandwich—
          a beautiful, golden-brown.

She catches my eye.
      "Perfect!"

RAIN

Not even cold rain
can get me down.
I shake it off,
join the masses in the hall,
hold onto the tiny hope
that the perfection I felt yesterday
means more
than just a golden-brown sandwich.

OUR CLASS PRESENTATION

The silent classroom,
stale air,
blank stares from classmates,
and Mr. Lewis's expectant expression
cause a logjam
inside my throat.

I glance at Zoe,
who leads me, with the curve of her smile,
to waist-deep grass,
autumn sunshine,
the scents of little bluestem, wild bergamot,
and sweet black-eyed Susan.

I switch my focus to the colors
of the clippings converging
on the curves of dry wood,
remember what we planned to talk about.

My words slowly meander,
intertwine with Zoe's.
My feet settle like deep roots.

AFTER CLASS

"We rocked that!"
Zoe grins from ear to ear.

I want to scoop her up
spin her around
shout.

I don't.

She asks if I want to meet at Compass Café
on Saturday to celebrate.
I answer, "Yes,"

wanting to repeat,
Yes, yes, yes, and *yes* again.

AT COMPASS CAFÉ

A woman with a head of white curls
stands in line before us,
peering into the pastry case.

She wears a paint smock
with the saying,
>Paint Your Dreams Come True!
and in larger letters,
>Bella's Studio,
the same logo painted on the window next door—
an art studio and gallery.
Could this woman be Bella?
I show Zoe, and she smiles, nodding.

The woman says, more to herself than the cashier,
>"I can't decide between the apple
>or the pumpkin."
She laughs, then turns to Zoe and me.
>"Missed opportunities
>are the ones we regret most."
To the cashier,
>"I'll take one of each.
>Save myself a trip later."

Pastry bag in one hand,
cup of coffee in the other,
she smiles wide at us,
all twinkling eyes.
          "Have a wonderful day!"

Standing next to Zoe,
it already is.

ALL WE CAN DO

Over the sound of the espresso machine
all we can do is look at each other.

It's nice.
Zoe smiles. I smile.

Zoe's fingers tap the side of her mug.
Maybe she wants to reach for my hand.

I wish she would.
I casually push my mug across the table

Our knuckles nearly touch.
When they finally do, a jolt

runs up my arm.
She smiles. I smile.

WINDING TOWARD THE CREEK

Zoe is a step ahead
laughing, leading, hips swaying
Hair, a maze in sunlight—
red and golden threads

Barely believing my luck,
wanting to make this moment last

my fingers brush along the base of a hickory—
shaggy bark, rough and dry—
catch
on a long curl
release it
before it snaps.

Zoe reaches back, takes my hand,
follows the scent of silt.

We slide   Pause   Slide   Pause
Down the steep slope
        to the edge of the creek,
        to my rock.
        Now ours.

KISSING

Zoe's usual need to twist words into long strings
washes away.

She leans so close, her freckles blur.
The afternoon fills with her lips on mine.

I am a quaking leaf in sunlight,
rooted to this moment.

3:21 p.m.

School is finally over, and I'm rushing
down the hall to meet Zoe,
ready to return to the creek just like we planned.
Itching to go. Itching
to kiss her again.

But at Zoe's locker
I find her sorting pens by color.
She doesn't look up.
          "Why didn't you tell me?"

I tighten my grip on my backpack.
"Tell you what?"

Her glance gives it all away.
In an instant I know I'm lost.
She says it:
          "Your mom died?"

Words I'd meant to say.
Words I couldn't.

"Who told you?"

She faces me, distrust swimming in her eyes.
        "My mom.
        Said someone at her work mentioned it.
        Seemed to think I should already know."

I pound the locker next to Zoe's.
Turn away.
Walk.

        "Wait!"
her voice trails after me,
        "Were you *ever* going to tell me?"

I don't stop.

SILENCE

Next few days
slip by
like summer did—
silently.

Part of me likes it that way.

I don't want to talk about what happened.
Don't want to relive the pain.
Don't want anyone else to talk either.
It's no one's business.

FOUR OAKS

On the ride up my grandparents' long driveway,
we come around a bend, see four beloved friends.
Strong as ever.
They're older than any wrinkled relative,
and I share more memories with them than
anyone
besides Mom.

I recall their earthy scent,
remember the years before Mom and I moved,
being so close
        to those four oak trees.

Baby photos of me show Mom lifting my hand
to reach their bending branches, ragged bark.
I used to race around their wide trunks,
catch grasshoppers, watch ants,
lean against them, underneath their shade,
as I sketched in a notebook.
Those trees talked and listened
in ways no human could.

I stuffed my pockets full of acorns.
Grandpa laughed,

said I was the luckiest girl in the whole county.
Explained that having an acorn in your pocket
brings good luck.
Mom taught me to plant them.

Ever since we moved off the farm,
"Home for Thanksgiving"
meant walking down to those four oaks
with Mom.
Hands wrapped around
insulated mugs of hot apple cider,
our warm breath escaping in white swirls,
we'd marvel at diamonds in the night.
The great hunter, *Orion*.

    "I could walk down with you,"
Daniel offers. Points his chin to the trees.

I'm surprised that he remembers.
Kindness in his voice makes me want to say, *yes*.

The word doesn't come.

He steers around another bend.
      "Or if you prefer to go alone, that's okay."

Is that what I want?
To go alone?

Canada geese fly south
in V-shaped formation, their calls
sounding mournful, but they
fly together.

WINTER

Days and nights
become muffled
muted
like the sounds of town
after the first snowfall.

I trudge through December
then January.
Just another body
moving through the hallways
sitting through classes
pushing my pen across the page.

With the change of semesters
Zoe slips into different classrooms
out of view.
I let her messages add up
until they stop.
Occasionally, I see her in the halls,
catch her eyes catching mine.
I strain against my body's natural current.
Turn away.
Urge my feet
to move faster.

Even as February
shows early signs of thaw,
I cannot get out the words
to explain.

I stay cold
numb,
even as days grow longer.

THE NIGHTMARE RETURNS

White lace curtains
Cherry blossoms

I scream…

Awake
my body stays flat.

Tears stream down.
Soak my pillow.

If it could,
love would walk across this silence,
wouldn't it?

CHIPPING AT ICE

The scene at Zoe's locker
stays frozen in my memory.

Using a walking stick
I claimed from the woods
I chip at the iced-over creek.
Chip at that remembered pity.

I chip at it, wishing to see
what might have been below.
What Zoe might have said,
had I not walked away.

I chip at my own silence.
Pound the ice.
Castigate myself until
the stick breaks ice.
Smashes into water.
Out of breath,
I stop.   Listen.
Hear the *chick-a-dee-dee-dee*.

PROJECT

Mr. Lewis stops me in the hall.
Says to take home my project.

The decoupage log.

It's been on display, but now he needs that space
for this semester's work.
Gripping my books tightly in front of me,
I stall by saying,
"It's not just mine."

But he tells me that Zoe
already said to give it to me.

It was Zoe's bright idea
to save that log from decomposing,
to turn our Ecology project into an art installation.

Why would she give it up?

But as soon as I think the question, I know—
she's given up on me,
and why wouldn't she?

CERAMICS

This semester
my elective is ceramics.
I like the way
the clay resists my palms
as I wedge—
knead it into readiness,
pound out air pockets,
form it into a ball.

HOW MISS COOPER TEACHES

When Miss Cooper lectures,
she keeps moving
clay in her hands
whether at the table or on the wheel.
Her words become motions,
or her motions become words.
I'm not sure which.

I'm transfixed.

From day one, we're given clay—
told to push, pull, roll, mold, add, subtract.

At the wheel,
while clay spins in her hands, she tells us,
it is up to us
to change the shape of our clay.
It's as much about carving out space
as the forms we build,
the balance between
space and matter,
like a page holding a poem,
space around the words
as important

as the words themselves,
in music, the silence
around a music note,
just as a good conversation
means listening
as well as talking.
That's what it's all about, she says—
conversations
between us and our art.

IT'S ABOUT LEARNING

…what to make the space for.
…where we want to stretch the clay.
…how far to push or pull,
and the exact moment
to do one
or both.
…what we choose to scrap,
or merely scrape away.
…when and where to add.
…how to put back.

Each of us
must find our own way.

Miss Cooper can show us techniques.
We can build skills.
But no one
can tell us what must come next.

> "It's up to *you*
> to decide."

A shiver runs through me.

MESSY

"Sometimes life gets messy
before it can take shape."
Miss Cooper looks at all of us
sitting on our stools like lumps of clay.
"Am I right, people?"

We know the drill by now.
We shout back, "Right!"

"Then get to work!
And make it messy!"

I splat my clay onto the bat.
Get the wheel up to speed.
Dribble water between my fingers
over the mound.
Embrace the slipperiness.
It's a tricky balance
between holding on
and letting go.

A DEAL

Miss Cooper offers me a deal.
If I help her
clean the art room after school,
I can get extra practice on the wheel,
working between the last bell of the school day
and when she goes home.
I don't blink before answering, *Yes!*

DAILY PRACTICE

Clay wicks away
the moisture in my hands
as well as doubting voices in my head.

Learning to center
becomes my only purpose.
Holding steady, pushing, pulling.

One nudge too far   everything falls.

Miss Cooper flashes the lights—
my cue to scrape up wet clay,
toss it into the slop bucket.
I marvel at how easy it is
to let go of the product
when my only focus
lies in the process.

Lathering lotion over my cracked skin,
I slowly bend and fold
one hand into the other.

Dry creases tell my story.

IN THE BASEMENT

I search through stacks of clutter,
piled up boxes

until my hands land on
one of Mom's college textbooks:
The Potter's Complete Handbook.

Just as I used to do, I slowly page through
step-by-step instructions
shown in black and white photographs.

Finally standing,
book tucked under one arm,
I'm drawn through the dim light
toward the lit stairway
but then, a reflection piques my curiosity.
I maneuver around more piles to get closer.

It's a dress
on top of a stack of clothes.
As soon as I touch it,
memories flood.

THE DRESS

Shortly after Mom died,
Daniel put her clothes in the basement.
Said I could sort through them,
have any I wanted.
The rest would go to charity.

The heap
stays untouched,
draped over the old brown chair.

When Mom became too weak
to walk up the stairs to the bedroom,
we set up a bed on the main floor.
To make space,
we pushed the old piano into one corner
and moved the brown chair down here.
It sits beside a box of old photographs
and the exercise ball no one used more than once.
Daniel's trombone is down here, too,
because his and Mom's jamming days
are long over.

I was furious
when he stuck her clothes down here in the dark.

Thought he was getting greedy for closet space.
Wondered why he was in such a rush.
I couldn't bear to look at—let alone touch—
her clothes.
It felt like losing her all over again.

I realize now
that maybe he felt that way, too,
every day getting dressed, her clothes beside his.

My pulse quickens as I lift
the silver-blue dress.
The one Mom wore
the night Daniel proposed.
The night he said
what an honor it would be
to become a family.
He said he understood
that at my age,
having a guy around the house
might take some getting used to.
I was ten.
Old enough to know
I was okay without a dad,
but young enough to enjoy having one.

Mom wouldn't say yes
until I did.
She put a lot of faith in me.
I see that now.
Grandma would say *pressure*.
That was Mom
doing things her own way.

It had always been just
Mom and me.
Until Daniel.

Watching the light reflect off the shiny fabric,
I carry the dress upstairs.
It's not the kind of thing I'd want to wear.
But that memory is too important
to give away.

DANA

I pull the clay too far, nick the side—
and, just like that, my pot crumples.
Letting the wheel wind down,
I hear the girl beside me:
      "No, no, nooo!"
Dana's pot wavers, wobbles,
and collapses too.
      "Crap."

I scrape up my clay,
hold the sloppy mess in my hands,
and catch Dana's eye.
She's been in my class since kindergarten,
but we've never really talked.
Don't know what makes me do it,
but I give her a flicker of a smile.

She glances from me to the clay in my hands,
then back to her own pot.
      "Brynn, how do you stay so calm?"

I shrug.
Don't admit that a collapsed pot feels small
next to all the other things in my life fallen apart.

Dana says,
> "Me? I want it perfect
> the first time, every time.
> It never is.
> But you? You just go with it,
> as if it's no big deal."

I chuckle. "It's not really. Look, I'll show you."
I lead her to the table in the center of the room,
repeat the motions Miss Cooper showed us.

All it takes to remedy this so-called tragedy
is more time,
steady hands,
wedging on a bit of canvas.

As we work our clay back into shape,
we keep talking.

BREAKING ROUTINE

It's nearing the end of February,
dreary with dirty snow and gray skies,
and I'm getting desperate to escape
my usual stuck-in-the-cold routine

when Dana suggests we go to Compass Café.

Normally, during this weather,
I trade going to the creek
for sitting in my room,
clipping words and photos,
arranging, and getting sticky with glue.

But my skin crawls with craving—

I want to shake something loose, set it free.
Not knowing what,
I agree to go,
because, at least, it'll be something different.

FRIENDSHIP

After school,
when Dana's done with jazz band, she meets me
in the ceramics room.
We walk to Compass Café.

Dana is quiet like me
but together
we have plenty to talk about.

It's not like it was with Zoe.
There's no *zing* pinging
through my body. Besides,
I've heard all about her crush on Frank,
the boy who sits next to her in band.

Friendship
is exactly what I want.
What I've missed.

LITTLE BY LITTLE

I stumble upon a truth risen from down deep
like a piece of limestone in a farmer's field,
moved to the surface
by constant freezing and thawing.

I want to tell someone.

       About Mom.
       Zoe.
       Everything.

I want someone to hear me.

I can't explain the change.
Perhaps time
has softened the sharp edges around me.

Whatever the reason, my story unfurls.
Setting words free
is like breaking through ice in the creek,
wedging clay,
making me new.

SWAPPING TALES

Dana grins and tells me that in band today,
she and Frank
shared some promising smiles.
Then she moans.
She still has no clue how to ask him out.
But the worst part is Erik,
the boy who sits on her other side.
He flirts so much,
Dana ends up flirting back.
She's sure both boys
will come to the wrong conclusion.

She knows she needs to make a move,
but she argues,
      "If Frank is actually interested in me,
      wouldn't he say something?"

I answer, "Maybe *he's*
thinking the same exact thing."

She arches one eyebrow,
smirks.
It's her way of recognizing
I make a fair point.

And also, that, maybe, I
should take my own
advice.

I arch my eyebrow back,
say, "Touché."
We laugh.

We're both stuck
in our inability to act,
to speak.

But somehow, talking about it
helps things make more sense.
Dana doesn't shake her head
or shame me
for being the screw-up I know I am.

We just sit
with what's happened,
with what is.

ANNOUNCEMENT

Miss Cooper calls for our attention.
    "I'm happy to announce
    that the public library
    will be hosting a student art show
    during the month of May.
    All students in Drawing and Painting
    as well as Ceramics I and II
    will participate.
    At a reception for the community,
    each of you will have a few minutes to talk
    about your piece on display.
    Be thinking
    about which piece
    you'd like to show
    and what you'd like to say about it.
    Any questions?"

Dana raises her hand.
    "Do we *have* to show something?"

Miss Cooper nods.
    "I'm hoping everyone
    will see this as an opportunity to grow.
    It's not a competition.

It's about sharing your art
and your process.
To show the larger community that art
has an important role in society."

A boy in the back cries out,
    "Will there be food?"
A ripple of laughter crosses the room.
Miss Cooper's eyes tease.
    "Yes, Andrew, there will be *light*
    refreshments.
    Now, get to work!"

SPINNING

An art show at the library
is just the kind of thing Mom
would've arranged.

She didn't, of course.

The thought of being there,
standing in front of everyone
brings black spots to my vision.

It won't be my pottery
but my grief
on display.

I catch myself before I fall.

Dana reaches out.
    "You okay?"
I nod. Try to shake it off.

BARN TALK

I'm in the barn handing tools to Grandpa
as he fixes the snowblower,
the smell of motor oil
mixing with the scent of hay.
It's been years
since my grandparents kept animals.
Years since storing hay.
But some things linger.

Grandpa wipes grease off a wrench,
        "Brynn, I've got to tell you…"
then wipes grease from his hands,
        "…we can't keep going on this way."
I tense, feeling the weight of his words,
figuring he means I need to decide
about Mom's ashes.
Grandma probably put him up to it.

It's worse.
        "We've decided to sell the farm."

The world seems to tilt and slide.
"What?" I stand, unsteady, my voice strangled.
"You can't."

He holds up a hand as if to stop me.
"Now, Brynn, just sit and hear me out."
That's the last thing I want, but I take a seat.
"We're not as young as we once were.
These two years—well,
they've taken a toll on us."
He rubs his knee, shoulders slump.
It's the first time I really see just how
bone-tired he looks.
"And your mother's medical bills….
Daniel's been doing the best he can,
but…."
He wipes the sweat from his brow, licks his lips.
"Well, something's got to be done.
Your grandma and I won't stand by
and watch the whole ship go down.
We don't have anything but this land,
so that's what we're going to do."

"But…." Panic grips. Twists.

He sighs.
"Truth be told,
we should've sold years ago.
It's too much to manage, even with

the neighbors doing the farming,
                just keeping after the snow and mowing."
He scowls at the dirt floor.

I shake with adrenaline.
"But this is the family home—five generations!"

He looks up.
        "I'm sorry, Brynn. I know.
        I know you love the farm, but
        family comes first."

"Exactly," I stomp my foot. "Family first!"
Tears turn my voice ragged. "This land
…*is* our family—
Don't you get it? All those years Mom taught me
to talk to trees, listen to the creek—
doesn't any of that matter?
We couldn't save Mom, but…?"
I picture the farm ripped apart,
replaced by houses and strip malls.
"You can't. You just can't!"

Grandpa takes hold of my shoulders,
tries to calm me.
        "Now, Brynn—"

But I won't hear it. Won't wait.

I tear away from him, take off
to the end of the driveway,
keep running down the road.

BLIND

> *I'll get through this,*
Mom assured me a year ago.
> *You'll see.*

But I didn't

        see.

ALONG THE ROAD

My lungs are raw from the cold air.
Daniel's truck rolls up beside me,
the passenger window already down.
        "Hey, Brynn. Grandpa called."
Too tired to keep going, I climb in.
The truck gets up to speed.   I ask

"Did you know?
That they plan to sell the farm?"

Daniel glances at me, then back at the road.
        "They mentioned the idea."

A numbing sensation moves through my body.
"Mom's medical bills…?"
Daniel runs his hand through his hair,
sighs heavily.

I recall the stacks of envelopes
stamped with "OVERDUE."
"It's true, then? It's that bad?"
My throat tightens.

Daniel clenches the steering wheel.

"I didn't want to worry you, but
                we could lose the house."
Lose the house? My mind reels.
It's one more punch to my stomach.

But losing the house would be nothing
compared to losing the farm.
I glare at him, grit my teeth. "Did you
tell them to sell?"

It catches him off guard.
        "No, of course not."
But I'm no longer listening. I need someone
to blame.
"You can't make them!
It's not even your family!"

It's only the countryside
rushing past my window,
but it's as though my life is sliding
out of my grasp.
"You have no right—"

Daniel raises his voice to cut me off,
        "Brynn,
        I did no such thing."

170

He pulls to the side of the road, parks.
His voice softens.
          "I would never…."

"Then, why?   Why would they—"

Daniel takes a deep breath. Exhales.
          "It sounded as though your grandparents
          have considered this
          for quite some time."

I wipe my wet cheeks. "But if I lose the farm—"
My words catch. I don't say

I'll lose myself.

LUCKY

March wind
is a pacing lion
outside Compass Café.

Inside,
it's packed.

Dana and I are lucky
to snag the last open table,
which is awkwardly close
to the side counter
with the napkin dispenser
and used-dishes bucket.

It'll have to do.

SECOND CHANCE

Another gust sweeps through the open door,
bringing Zoe, windswept and rosy.

I nearly duck under the table,
but Dana smacks my arm.
        "Go talk to her!"

Zoe waits in line to order,
not talking to anyone.
But what would I say?

I indicate my full latte to Dana and shrug,
meaning, *Case closed.*

Her brow furrows. She gets up,
grabs her notebook and backpack,
puts her mug into the bucket, says with a wink,
        "See ya, Brynn,"
leaving me alone in the crowd.

Aiming to make my own quick exit
but too flustered
        to do so gracefully,
I knock over my drink   watch

as it seeps into my Algebra 2 notebook.

Springing for the napkin dispenser,
I nearly crash into Zoe.
        We freeze.
She laughs, and her voice comes out friendly.
        "We've got to stop meeting like this."

It's a corny line, and she knows it,
the sparkle in her eyes invites me to volley next.

"Uh, yeah," I laugh, but it stumbles,
not sure where to go.
I remember the spill   my homework.
        I blink,
wipe up the mess, then ask, "Meeting someone?"

I consider giving her my table,
slinking out without a shred of dignity.

She shakes her head.
        "Just doing homework."

Surprising myself,
I point to the seat across from mine.
"Join me."

174

ACROSS THE TABLE

Zoe conjugates Spanish verbs.
I recopy algebraic expressions.
Tensions begin to thaw.

UPDATE

"So…give me the rundown!"
Dana insists as we walk to lunch.
"What happened with Zoe?"
I elbow her in the side, "I can't believe
you just left me there!"
But I smile, and the longer she watches me,
waiting,
the more I blush,
until I'm laughing, because
she's now bouncing instead of walking.
"See! I told you!
You just had to make a move!"
"Well," I laugh, shrugging. "It might be a start."
At our table, Dana bites into her apple,
a far-off look in her eyes.
I ask, "Did you
talk to Frank yet?"
She snorts, shakes her head.
"Come on, Dana, if I can do it, so can you.
Promise me," I snatch one of her chips,
"…this afternoon, you're going to say *hello*
and ask about his day."

FLAWED

In ceramics, I remind Dana of her promise, but
she's too frustrated about her pot from the kiln.
> "How am I supposed to make something
> for the Art Show?
> All my stuff comes out looking lumpy and
> crooked!
> Even the colors I chose are ugly.
> Why bother making anything?
> I can buy something so much better
> from a store."

Miss Cooper is walking by. She stops.
Addresses the class.
> "Dana brings up an interesting question.
> Is the goal
> to recreate something that looks
> store-bought?"

No one answers.
Miss Cooper continues.
> "Not in this class.
> Make your pottery your own—
> let it be real and flawed
> and wonderful.
> The beauty is in that touch of humanity.

The only way to grow as a potter—
and a person—
is to embrace who we really are,
and our pottery is part of that.
Until we do that,
we'll never get anywhere."

Dana rolls her eyes, as if to say,
Miss Cooper is on her soapbox again.

But I like what she's saying. I think more about it
as I work and rework my clay.

STILL EMPTY

Closing the door on the wind,
I am hit by the stillness inside our house.
Dark and dusty
cluttered
empty.

My stomach growls.

Dropping my school bag on the floor,
I step out of my winter boots,
head to the fridge.

Find it, also,
empty.

PING

I zip my coat,
slip back into my winter boots,
walk two blocks to Monty's Mini Mart.

A pretzel bag under one arm,
I'm filling a cup at the fountain drink machine
when my phone pings.

Switching the cup to my left hand,
I take out my phone, swipe without looking.
At this time of day, it can only be Dana.
I don't even read the message before tapping out,
>   *Talk to Frank?*
because I'm not letting her out of her promise.

Waiting for her answer,
I sip raspberry iced tea.

Another ping.

I nearly choke
when I notice the messages aren't
from Dana.

THEY'RE FROM...ZOE

I quickly scroll up, reread the first message:
> *At Compass Café.*
> *Want 2 come?*

The second reads:
> *Frank who?*

My face feels hot. I punch at the keys:
> *Sorry, never mind.*

Then:
> *Be there soon.*

IN LINE

Waiting to pay for my raspberry tea and pretzels,
I'm standing behind a man, who takes his time
with every step.
He wears an old John Deere cap.
He slides his money across the counter,
asks the cashier,
    "Ready for the big snow?"
The cashier shakes her head.
    "Oh, please, don't you start!
    Radio said nothing but a dusting."
The man shrugs,
dropping the change into his pocket.
    "Wouldn't be so sure.
    Wouldn't be the first time
    these old bones
    disagreed with a weatherman."
He laughs, shaking a knobby finger at her.
    "You be careful out there."
Out the window, the sky is clear blue.
Trees sway in the wind, but any snow
must be a long way off.

SOMETHING WILD

Walking up Main Street, I spot Zoe
waiting outside Compass Café.
It takes only a moment until she notices
and rushes over to me.

      "Let's go somewhere else.

      Let's go *do*

      something. Something wild."
Her eyes search mine.
Like I'll come up with some amazing
plan.
Right.
Why don't I write *boring* on my forehead?

Her eyes light up.

      "We can go to my house!"
She links arms with me, starts walking.
My feet drag. I remember Kim's cool,
calculating eyes.
"Wait—what about your mom? Would she
…be okay with that?"

Emotions flash across Zoe's face.
Worry? Panic?
She checks her watch.

"We've got a good two hours.
But let's come back before six o'clock.
My mom's picking me up."
I raise an eyebrow—*Why not just stay home?*
She waves away my unspoken question.
"You know how she gets.
She'll be mad if I'm not here."

"Then let's stay here."

She wrinkles up her nose.
"I want to do something different.
Anyway,
you've never been to my house."
Her eyes plead. She tugs my arm.
"I promise,
it'll be fun!"

AT THE EDGE OF TOWN

Zoe lives in an old farmhouse. A cornfield
stretches to the east,
but we climb a bluff that looks to the west,
and from up here I notice that a strong wind
has swept in a long line of coal gray clouds.
Zoe pulls her knitted cap
low over her ears.
I pull my hat from my pocket, do the same.
We catch our breath, take in the view.
Snow-covered hills,
patches of bare trees,
distant hills that blur into sky.
Layers of white, gray-brown, and frosty blue.

ATOP THE BLUFF

I wonder what we're doing
but know better than to ask.
I made her wait by the creek,
so I wait.
Watch.

Zoe holds a challenge in her eyes,
faces the wind and clouds,
extends her arms wide,
breathes in.

Twirling fast,
she unleashes a scream.
Long.
Loud.
Lovely.

MY TURN

Zoe winds down,
comes to a full-stop.

Cheeks flushed,
she grabs my hands—
    "Your turn!
      Scream as loud as you can!"

We twirl
fast, faster!

Our voices fling in every direction.

IT'S FUNNY

Being loud
feels so freeing—
making sound from deep down inside my belly
and letting it fly
for no good reason.

ALCOVE

Zoe leads me
to an alcove in the limestone outcrop.
We fold our bodies tight into the space,
out of the wind.

SHE TELLS ME

Sometimes she sings here
the echoes of her own voice
the only reminder
she has one.

STONE

She picks up a small stone
from the ledge beside her.
Puts it in my hand.
Tells me
she still has the rock I gave her.

I feel the stone—
one sharp edge,
the rest, smooth.

WHAT'S GOING ON?

Ever since we left Compass Café,
it's like she's been full of words
she's not spilling.

INSIDE

We hang our coats on hooks in the entryway,
kick off boots, and Zoe loses her balance.
I catch her elbow but instead of steadying her,
she lands up against me, laughing into my ear.
Our eyes lock and then all is quiet
except for a grandfather clock
ticking away seconds.

It's just us, but she whispers,
as though the empty parlor might hear,
     "May I kiss you?"

There's so much we haven't said,
so much in the air we haven't cleared

but I want this electric charge
to finally strike ground.
"Yes," I whisper.

Zoe cups my jaw,
pulls me to her mouth—warm and urgent.
I am lost in the heat of her hands
that reaches down to my bones.

HER IDEA

Zoe leads me upstairs to her bedroom
in the back corner of the house.
I stumble after her, dizzy with desire.
She stops, turns, and blushes.

Does she feel as awkward as I do?
Here. Suddenly. In her room.
Knowing what, at least, I think,
we plan to do next.
Is she doubting her idea?
Is she as clueless as I am?
Does she know how
to get from here
to there?

SITTING ON THE EDGE OF THE BED

Zoe twines her fingers through mine.
      "You ever do this before?"

Heat rushes to my face.

      "It's okay,"
she says quickly.

I ask, "You?"
She looks past my shoulder.
      "I messed around some
      with a girl at my old school, but
      she never wanted to be seen together.
      One day, it was just over."

Her pause seems to ask
if I plan to stick around.

I lean in. Kiss her softly.

SAFE WITH ZOE

Between flannel sheets
our hands roam
over and under
loosened clothes.
Drift over skin.
We say nothing.
Just breathe in rhythm
together.

SURPRISE ARRIVAL

The moment the front door slams
Zoe's body
tries to move in three different directions.
     "It's not even five o'clock!"
She scrambles to get her sweater back on.

Below,
her mother shouts:
     "Zoe McClain,
     get down here!"

I fumble with shirt buttons,
ask, "What should I do?"

Zoe swings the door open.
     "Come on."

FOLLOWING

Heart racing, I pause
at the end of the hallway,
still out of sight,
but Zoe must be downstairs
because Kim's voice shrieks.

      "How could you *do* that to me?

      "Why haven't you answered your phone?

      And *whose* coat is that?"

I swallow my fear,
take the stairs fast,
catch myself
before bumping into Zoe at the bottom.

Her mother's eyes widen,
then narrow into darts aimed straight at me.
      "*You.*"

ONE WORD

Zoe can only say one word:

> "I…I…"

Kim has so many more:

> "Do you even understand
> what you've done?
> Zoe—that internship
> was going to set you on track
> for college admissions."

Zoe tries again.

> "But Mom, I don't want—"

Kim's not done:

> "What other opportunities
> do you think this Podunk town
> is going to offer you?"

The room begins to spin.
Something about that word—*internship*—
feels familiar. But why?

Trying to steady myself,
I hold onto the banister,
listen to Kim's boots pace the hardwood floor.

> "Connie called me to let me know
> you didn't show.

Zoe, you don't just blow off an interview.
Especially when it's with my boss.
Reputation is everything in a small town!
And now
I find you here
with *her?*"

All of Zoe's words
dry up.

I wish I could shrink and disappear
        into the microscopic strands
                of a piece of orange lint
                        stuck to Zoe's sweater.

Boots stop,
Kim's voice shoots straight into me:
        "Did you
        put her up to it?
        What are you even doing here?"

QUESTIONS

Like an antique typewriter
my mind gets jammed.
Too many keys
pressed at once.

GUILTY AS CHARGED

I blink
barely breathe
want to object.
My jaw hangs open
unable to form a single word.
I watch how quickly
in her eyes
my silence
becomes proof.

THE SUM OF HER WORDS

Kim draws in a breath through her nose,
lets it out fast.
    "Listen,
    I understand
    this has been a tough year for you."
My body goes rigid.
No way is she talking about my mom.
No way.   Not now.
    "I'm very sorry for your loss."
I want to scream. Scream at her to mind her *own*
business.
Scream at Zoe to say *something*.
Scream to the sky and hills.
All I do
is stand and watch Kim's expression harden.
    "But I will not
    let you drag Zoe down with you.
    You roam about, going nowhere.
    You're nothing
    but a waste of her time."

OUT OF THERE

I push past Zoe
her mom
grab my coat and hat
stomp into my boots
swing open the door
cross the weathered porch
pick up speed

NOISE

A harsh wind
roars between angry tossed-about trees,
but even all that noise
can't drown out Kim's words—
cold bullets
to my heart.

You're nothing....

MORE THAN EVER

I need quiet
More than ever
I wish Mom were in the woods
waiting
to hear me

THROUGH TOWN AND BEYOND

Hot shame is the blade to my cheek
prodding my feet to pound pavement
storm through prairie
run until I'm thick between the trees.

I leap across the creek
climb
crawl
claw
up to the ridge
down.

There's no path anymore
just my feet plowing
up and over these hills.

If I'm nothing but a waste of time to Zoe,
nothing worth defending,
I might as well go
nowhere
fast.

ONWARD

Flurries lick the warmth of my face.
I push on.

ROAMING

Roaming has always been my way.
Before Mom got sick   during
and now.   That's who I am.
I will not be bound to a yard,
a tidy, well-lit street designed by someone else.
Does that give Kim the right
to berate me?
Does it make me unworthy?
Because I find more comfort among trees
than a room full of people?
What I know
are these two feet of mine.
What I know
is this earth beneath me.
I know that if I head north,
following the lichens
on the northside of tree trunks,
just as my mother taught me,
I'll come to my grandparents' farm,
to the back woods,
where Mom and I used to roam together.

SOON ENOUGH

A part of me believes
I'll find her,
if only I can get there
soon enough.

CHANGES

Flurries join tip to tip,
turn into wet, lazy snowflakes.

These are the best
for catching.

    Stick out your tongue, Brynn,
my mom used to say.

I don't stop.

FENCE

The boundary between the county park
and my grandparents' farm

is an old tattered fence,
a "No Trespassing" sign

a harvested cornfield beyond,
staccato beige lines poking through snow.

I swing my legs over the fence,
plant my feet in that field.

THE VALLEY

Walking across this open space
exhausts me.
I'm exposed, and the other side
suddenly feels too far to reach.
Cornstalks, left after harvest
half-covered in snow,
trip my feet, tire me out.

I stop in the middle,
gaze
at the falling snow,
muted lines of trees
on distant hills.

For one slow-moving moment
I catch my breath

only to have it knocked right out again
as a sweeping wind, so fierce,
pushes me down.

UNFAMILIAR GROUND

Cut open with rage
I yell as though the wind could listen

but not only does the wind offer no apology,
it steals my voice.

Destroys my sense of direction
as sky and ground unite,
become rolling waves of snow.

GO AHEAD

Erase me

like every tree
hill

hope

IN THE MIDDLE

The thing is

when caught in a snowstorm

an open field is not
a safe place to stop. No matter how much
I want
to shut down.   My body
moves without asking.   Breathes
breath after breath

Muscles shiver
Teeth chatter

It takes more effort
to keep still.   My feet
pick a direction,   walk

step after step

OUT OF REACH

A mess of thorned brambles snag at my clothes.
Deeper in, the trees quiet the wind.
I get my bearings. Locate north.

But the cold reminds me to get real—even if
I walk all the way to the back woods, I know
Mom won't be there. My fingers

fumble, dig
into my pocket, pull out my phone.
No signal. Low battery. I turn the power off,
stow it. Turn west.

MESSAGES WAITING

Atop the ridge is my best chance
for getting phone signal.
I climb and keep on
until I reach the road.

I switch on the power. Wait.
Watch the logo dance
across the screen. Wait again.
Three out of four bars appear. Eight
missed calls, four
voicemails, three
texts.

Before I can think,
hope rockets through me, hope
that Zoe
has tried to reach me

But they're all from Daniel and Grandma.

I MAKE THE CALL

Daniel's breathless panic
shakes me.
  "Brynn—are you okay?
  Where are you?"
Tears sting, but I manage
to say I'm fine.
Wind makes noise. He must know
I'm outside somewhere.
He says he'll come get me
but I'm embarrassed, afraid
to admit I'm stranded.
  "Please, Brynn."
His voice cracks, and in that sound, I hear
he's asking permission
to be my family.
  "Please tell me where you are."

ARRIVAL

I don't realize how much I want to see Daniel
until my heart leaps at the sight of his truck.
I wave him down.

The truck slows,
pulls to the side of the road
stops,
flashers on.

Like moths to a flame, snowflakes
fall across the headlights.
I squint at the brightness.

Daniel climbs down, walks around
the front of the truck, a silhouette,
arms stretching wide. I let myself
fall forward. Take in what's real.
The scratchy wool of his coat against my cheek,
throaty sound of the idling engine,
smell of exhaust,
the scent of wet snow.
He is here.
So am I.

WORRY

We're closer to the farm
so Daniel doesn't turn back toward town.
      "Your grandparents are worried sick.
      Didn't mean to worry them,
      but I didn't know who else to call."
Because of the snow, Daniel left work early.
When I wasn't at home, he called.
When I didn't pick up, he sent a text, warning me
about the snow coming. Call after call
didn't get through. Messages added up.
While I was in the valley with no signal,
they were at home,
weathering a different storm.

WHEN WE ENTER THE KITCHEN

Grandma and Grandpa hover
on either side
of an old, battered weather radio.

Grandma sees us first, springs from her chair,
wraps her arms tight around me.

Grandpa holds us both,
whispering something between a prayer
and reassurance,
        "She's all right. She's all right."

TAKING CHARGE

Grandma ushers the men out of the room,
orders me to take off my wet clothes.
　　　"Here, by the woodstove."
Drapes two quilts around my shivering body,
tucks me into a chair closest to the heat,
hands me a mug of hot tea,
rushes upstairs, brings down
a dry set of clothes.
　　　"When you're ready, help yourself."
Looking at my wet hair, she frowns.
　　　"Be right back."
She returns with a hairdryer,
runs her fingers through my short crop,
drying it quickly.
　　　"So much easier than your mom's."
She chuckles.
　　　"You drinking that tea?"
I nod. Take a sip.

NIBBLE

Grandma offers me food,
everything from graham crackers
to chicken noodle soup,
but all I want is sleep.
I nibble,
can hardly swallow.
Too many tears lodged in my throat.

SUNSHINE THROUGH MY WINDOW

I wake
to the smells of coffee and bacon,
morning sunshine filtered
through tiny shapes in cotton lace curtains.

Beneath thick layers
of Grandma's handmade quilts, I watch
the patterns of light and shadows
shift on the wall
as the curtains waver in the heat from the vent.

Mom and I
slept and played
in this same room,
a generation apart.

Grandpa said it so many times.
How could I forget?

> *My Grand-Pop built this ol' house*
> *with his own two hands.*
> *Built it to last. And it has!*
> *Five generations, counting you.*

BREAKFAST

My grumbling stomach urges me out of bed,
down the smooth-worn, creaky staircase
to the kitchen, where Grandma
is all alone, wiping the counter with a wet rag.
    "The guys are digging out Daniel's truck.
    You want breakfast?"
She barely waits for an answer,
    starts cracking eggs,
puts bread in the toaster.
    "Radio said we got eleven inches!"
she tells me, pouring a glass of orange juice.
    "The storm drifted further south
    than they'd expected,
    then stalled out."
She hands me the glass, checks the eggs.
    "At least it won't last long."
      She switches to buttering toast,
serves up the eggs,
    retrieves bacon from the oven,
      and sits across from me,
but her one-sided conversation
        keeps going....

SAME OLD, SAME OLD

>*She never stops.*

Back when my chin barely grazed the tabletop
sitting in this same chair,
I watched and listened to Grandma—a whirlwind
of motion, constant talking.   It exhausted me,
trying to keep up.
I grew up hearing that I should speak more,
speak louder.
But I could never get a word in edgewise.

She talks around me.

She talks until it becomes noise,
until I have nothing left to say
because by the time
there's a beat of silence that she thinks
I should fill,
I've cut up all my words,
separated them into different closed envelopes
inside my mind.
She doesn't wait long enough
to make space where I can paste my words
back together into something coherent.

DANIEL

During the drive back home
there's no
> *What were you thinking*
> *going into that snowstorm?*

No
> *How could you be so stupid?*

Daniel doesn't say
all the things I say to myself.

He doesn't say
anything.

THE NEXT MORNING

Instead of rushing off,
Daniel sits at the table
while I eat breakfast.
> "Brynn,
> I'd like to hire you
> to work at the nursery."

I stop chewing,
look up from my cereal.
He clears his throat.
> "Part time, of course.
> School comes first."

I chew again.
> "As you know, we're starting spring hours.
> I could use your help.
> And…"

his face softens,
> "it would be nice to have you around."

I wonder if that's the real reason he's asking.
Maybe he thinks he can keep a better eye on me.
But he doesn't make it sound like punishment.
I ask, "What would I do?"
He leans back in his chair.
> "Behind-the-scenes work—
> help in the greenhouse, plug trays,

fulfill mail orders, watering."

He knows I won't want to talk to customers.

I set down my spoon.

Think about the woods, the creek,

the freedom I've had.

The danger I got myself into.

The cost of coffee every week with Dana.

I agree.

AT LUNCH

Dana gives me the play-by-play
about how she and Frank finally talked
and how they're going bowling this Saturday night.

She worries it'll be embarrassing.
Renting those old shoes and all.
      "And I haven't bowled in six years.
      But who cares? I'll be with Frank.
      We have to do something, right?"
She bites into a carrot stick.

I can only muster a weak smile, but I do say
that I'm happy for her.
Don't say
that I'm wondering
whether anyone ever really gets a happy ending.

What if there are just fleeting blissful moments
that come crashing down
the moment we believe
something could go right for once?

I know how dreary my thoughts sound, so
I keep them to myself—

not wanting to dampen her excitement.

When the lunch bell rings,
Dana repacks her chips and carrot sticks.
        "You okay, Brynn?
        You're really quiet—even for you."
It's meant to be a friendly tease.
But I don't have an answer.

NOBODY

Nobody
knows what happened at Zoe's house.
Nobody
knows why I was out there in the storm.

I'm not sure if I'll be able to tell them,
but I feel the weight

of nobody asking.

I know why they don't—
      I'm always out roaming.
      Always not talking.

It's what they expect.

CAUGHT

Before I can get my books,
close my locker,
head down to the art room,
clear my head

Zoe slides up, desperate desire
flashing in her eyes.

I'm flooded with longing
to touch her hand,
smell her hair.

Zoe leans close.
      "I wanted to call you so bad.
      Mom yelled at me for hours."

Kim's voice comes sharp in my mind:
      Did you
      put her up to it?

Dread sinks its teeth into my skin.
I get the feeling that listening to Zoe
will make me look even more
like her accomplice.

Anger, like acid,
flickers up my throat.

If I had chosen to be her accomplice—
which I didn't
because I knew nothing of that interview—
I was the kind left at the scene of the crime.
Set up to be caught.

I DON'T ASK

Me:

Why didn't you tell me
about that interview?
Did you forget?

How could you forget
when your mom must've
reminded you
a million times that day?

Why did you even ask me
to come over?

I was stranded—

Zoe:

"I'm totally
grounded.
Mom took away
everything—
my phone,
computer."

"I'm not even
supposed to
talk to you."

"Total lockdown."

"But I had to see
you."

accused by your mom,
then the snowstorm.

She checks her
watch.

"Crap!"

She rushes
down the hall.

You set me up,
didn't you?

CUT

I slam my locker shut,
don't even go to the art room,
run all the way home,
a cold edge to the wind.

First thing I see when I round the corner
are those overgrown shrubs
blocking the front of our house—
those horrid yews
with their burnt orange badge
of January's deep-freeze.

Mom's plan was always
to cut them down.

I chuck my backpack at the porch,
climb over old junk in the shed, reach
for the loppers
and dive into those bulky branches.
I wrestle each one
like they are the words
I didn't say
to Zoe.

EVENING

I work until all that is left of those yews
are naked, awkward stubs,
sticking up through snow.
A sea of mixed green and burnt orange
around my legs.

I don't know what else to do
but stack the branches.
Leave them.

By the time Daniel's truck pulls into the driveway,
I'm eating a peanut butter & jelly sandwich
up in my bedroom. I move to the window.
Watch him step down,
pause in front of the pile,
then toss branch after branch
into the bed of the truck.

He climbs into the cab,
backs out slowly,
drives away.

When he returns,
he quietly goes to the kitchen.

Later, he stands in my doorway.
        "I took those branches
        to the village compost pile."

I don't blink. Only nod.
Hold my breath,
expect to hear
what a mess I've made of things.

        "Goodnight, Brynn.
        Get to bed soon."

I exhale. Whisper my thanks
a moment too late.

WINTER

MELTS

INTO

SPRING

SPRING EQUINOX

The last of melting snow
leaves behind
a flattened
bleached-out landscape.
Warm winds loosen,
kick up
autumn clutter,
reveal a wet layer.

UPDATE #2

"Hey, you want to eat outside?"
The temperature has climbed
to 72 degrees.
I follow Dana out to the school lawn.
Students sprawl everywhere, soaking up sunshine.
Dana offers me one of her chips.
"So, Frank and I are bowling again
this Saturday, and I thought
you could come, too, and…"
Her voice winds up like a game-show host.
She wiggles her eyebrows.
"…you could invite Zoe!
What do you think? Spring break!
Double-date?"
As far as Dana knows, Zoe and I haven't done anything
since that day we did homework together.
Now that things are progressing with Frank,
she must be more hopeful
about getting Zoe and me together.
"I can't—" I say, "It's my first day of work."
She blinks at me.
"You got a job?"
I tell her about Daniel's offer

246

and figure I've side-stepped the whole
"double-date" question
until she suggests,
          "Okay, then, Saturday *night*?
          Or another day?"
The weather is gorgeous,
and I want nothing more
than to lean back and enjoy it,
but words collect in the back of my throat
like heavy rainclouds.
Dana's eyes narrow.
          "What's up?"
I hesitate   then
let it all fall out,
"I don't think we'll be double dating
for a long time   if ever."
She groans.
          "What happened *now*?"
I spend the rest of lunch telling her.

FIRST DAY OF WORK

Daniel and I work side by side
saying only what needs to be said.

But it's a comfortable quiet.

Seeds we collected in autumn
have now grown into seedlings.

I'm in awe of these humble beginnings.

CLEAN SWEEP

I'm home for spring break,
and since Prairie Hill Nursery is closed
on Mondays,
Daniel is home, too.
But according to my grandparents
there will be no
idling away our time.

Eight in the morning,
Grandma knocks on the door,
bucket of cleaning supplies at her side.
Grandpa, armed with his toolbox,
is already set to work fixing the squeaky step.

He and Daniel go out to the shed,
pull everything out, start sorting,
then load up the truck with stuff to give away.

Grandma opens a window,
cries out

    "Make way for spring!"

I can't help laughing
even though, by now, my arms ache

from all the dusting
scrubbing
pounding out dirt.

All this cleaning seems to be shifting
the melancholy feeling that's held on
to every object in this house
and turned the air stale in each quiet room,
a stillness that Daniel and I haven't
been able to stir on our own.

In the backyard, we shake out the misery
clinging to our living room drapes.
I watch as dust lifts into the wind.
My heart lifts with it.

BASEMENT

Daniel sorts through boxes in the basement,
comes upstairs, wants my opinion.
      "What do you think about this?"
He holds up an electric mixer.
I shrug. "I always use a fork or spoon.
He sets it in the "Sell or Give Away" box.
      "And this?"
A stuffed animal I won at a county fair.
      "It can go."
Then he hauls up a huge box packed with old
magazines.
Grandma peers in, leaning on her broom.
      "For Pete's sake, your mother
      kept everything."
My heart races as though I see gold.
I twist the old saying, "One woman's trash
is another woman's treasure."
Grandma's doubt turns to a challenge.
      "Oh, really…?
      I want to see what you do
      with these."
Already,
my mind is clipping out words.

SCRUBBING

Grandma scrubs the grit
sticking to the floorboards in our entryway.
    "People just don't clean
    the way they used to.
    Not the down-on-your-knees,
    elbow-grease clean.
    They take the easy way out.
    It's too bad.
    They'll never know
    the fresh-start feeling that comes
    after a good spring cleaning."

I scrub at those same floorboards,
wondering why sometimes
it's so hard to put sponge to dirt.

It takes work to uncover truth,
to be willing to see what's real.

DUST TO DUST

I'm listening to Grandma's chatter
as I dust the bookshelves. Before I know it
my rag is next to the small wooden box.

All this time, I've kept my distance
knowing Mom's ashes are inside.
Now I'm up close.
I look at the crisscross pattern.
The light and dark strips of wood.
Imagine Nina's mom taking the time
to lay down each piece, puzzling it together.
Imagine the tears it took
to build a work of art for a dying friend.

It's not just a box but a labor of love.

WHERE I STAND

Grandma must notice
because her monologue takes a sharp turn—
the thawing ground, local farmers prepping fields.
Says it's about time we check the old cemetery,
our family plot,
see what cleanup is needed there.

She doesn't have to say
what's on the tip of her tongue.

I ignore the push. Realize this box
gave Mom a safe, beautiful place
to wait
until I became ready to stand,
walk again.

GEESE RETURNING HOME

I gaze out the open window
to the fixed porch step.
Think about all that my grandparents and Daniel
have done today to make this house feel better.
Not so empty.

A loud trumpeting sound draws my attention
to the sky
where a flock of Canada geese fly north

as if calling, "We're alive, we're alive,"
awakening the world to springtime.

A flutter of wings turns my focus back
to the porch.
The coo of a mourning dove.

All of us have weathered winter.

PRESCRIBED PRAIRIE BURN

My work today is to observe.

Daniel is leading a prairie burn
on a client's private property.
I'm not allowed to help because I'm a minor,
but he wants me to document what I see.
Take photos and write about the different jobs.

I watch from a nearby hill.

Before a single match is lit,
Daniel rechecks
air temperature, relative humidity, and wind speed.
Fence posts get sprayed with water.

Only after Daniel burns a small test fire
evaluates
and decides it's safe to go ahead,
does the crew spread out.

Some drip lines of fire from torches.
Others control the line.
Still more, mop up.

Flames fold thatch
like orange waves creeping down the slope.
Pink-white smoke
billows toward blue sky
and dry stalks licked by fire
burn to black ash.

PROOF

I was seven years old. Springtime.

Hand-in-hand, Mom walked me
to the north side of town
right up to the edge
where the restored prairie begins.

She had just shown me the new apartment
we'd be moving into. While she was excited
that I'd get to walk to school, all I could think
was that we'd be off the farm,
far from the four oak trees and back woods.

Why did Mom bring me here?
I wondered, looking at the desolate land
covered in black ash.
Mom leaned down,
bringing her face close to the ground.
>"The black ash absorbs sunlight
>and warms the ground.
>Then prairie plants
>send up new shoots."

I leaned down, too,
marveling at all the tiny green points

poking through the black.

Mom spoke to those sprouts
as though they were young children.
          "Welcome to spring, Little Ones."

She told me that people use fire
to burn away dry parts no longer living
while roots hold on below
alive and waiting.
          "I know this move is a big change.
          But I think these ashes and sprouts
          are proof that transitions—
          even those that appear destructive
          on the surface—
          can lay the ground for new growth."

Before we left that day,
she spoke again to the sprouts.
          "Keep on growing."

She kept bringing me back.
It's where she volunteered
and fell in love with Daniel.

Together, they taught me about stems and leaves

petals and seeds.
Introduced me to those plants that gradually grew
into my good friends.

COMPASS PLANT

Like hot flames, the reality of Mom's death
burns.

I lay down.
Look at the clear sky.

Can I
be like a compass plant?

Root deep.
Send up new growth.
Find the right direction.

LETTERS

Using Grandma's system for sorting mail,
I recycle and throw away
until I have only two items:

an electric bill with an overdue notice
an envelope addressed to me.

I drop the bill into the mail basket,
run up to my room,

slide my finger over graceful loops and curls.
Zoe's handwriting.

I imagine her hand
gliding the pen across the paper.

Inside
is a perfect, paper rectangle.
I unfold it carefully.

ZOE WRITES PLENTY

She describes feeling trapped
inside a small, boxed life
that her mother has designed.

How her days seem long without me.

That she's been reduced to writing snail mail
and has no idea how she'll get through
the rest of spring break.

My hope switches off
because
nowhere does she apologize or explain.

She writes, *I know I'm not supposed to talk to you
but I need to.*

I think about writing back:
How about listening for a change?

WHAT'S THE POINT?

I stare at that dot—the period—
at the end of her sentence
       I need to.
It's a smudge.
Blue ink against white paper.
I stop to wonder where it's going.
Floating in space?
Or taking root somewhere?
I wonder if that's like us.
Are we
floating apart?
Can we ever hope to take root?
She wants to talk, but
is there any point?

RECTANGLE

I refold her note.
Press my fingers
over every crease
until it's a perfect
rectangle.   Back
in the   envelope.

Does Zoe even realize
she should apologize?
Until she does, I don't
have anything   to say,
and   I   am   done
l i s t e n i n g.

NEWS

Daniel tears off a slice of garlic bread,
mops up the leftover sauce on his plate.
>"Your grandfather called today."
I twirl a large clump of spaghetti onto my fork,
shove it into my mouth.
>"The farmer next door,
>who's been renting their fields,
>sounds interested in buying."
My mouth is too full to speak.
We chew in silence. He finishes first,
swigs some water, then adds,
>"He even looked at the house."
I swallow. "What's he need a house for?
Hasn't he already got one?"
Daniel shrugs.
>"Maybe he'll rent it out."
The thought feels like a hammer
shattering me into pieces.
A warning whisper comes,
>*It's really happening.*

MY LOCKER

Anger and confusion are still brewing
as I wonder why Zoe invited me.
The moment I turn the corner
to the hallway of my locker
I see her waiting.

Our eyes lock.
She smiles.

I don't.
Without

the heart or stomach
to listen to her chatter, I

turn to the right, head straight
to class, glad that I'm only wearing
a sweatshirt and not a coat, grateful for
the one notebook in my bag.   Relieved
that I don't need to go to my locker   yet.

A LUMP OF CLAY

Dana is all business wedging
while I complain about Zoe and her letter.
I don't mention
the farm up for sale. Still can't say *that*
out loud.
Just poke at my lump of clay.

Dana looks at me hard.
          "Maybe you're better off without her."
She takes her smooth ball to a wheel,
gets it spinning.
I sit beside her.

"So, I should do nothing?"

Dana looks over.
          "Brynn,
          you were out in that blizzard
          because of her."

I slam my clay onto the bat.
"It's my own fault.
I should've gone home."

Dana lets her wheel wind down.
	"So, she's off the hook, then?"

I stare at my clay. It's nowhere near
ready to throw.

Dana snaps her fingers at me, spraying wet slop.
	"Brynn, wake up!
	She shouldn't've asked you over that day.
	She's the one who messed up.
	Not you.
	Her mom was way out of line.
	You didn't deserve any of that.
	And Zoe just let it happen."

I press on the foot pedal. The clay wobbles.
"I know.	But
do you think she did it on purpose?"

It's the question that keeps circling.

Dana shrugs.
	"Either way,

	she owes you an apology."

END OF CLASS

Miss Cooper stops me on my way out.
     "You aren't very far on your piece
     for the art show. Are you sure
     you still want to work on the wheel?"
Her eyebrows rise.
     "Today, you...."

"I know," I mumble,
focusing on the duct tape around my shoes,
"I'll work harder next time."

She sighs.
     "I'm staying late tonight after school.
     Can you be here?"
She's offering me an olive branch.

I nod.

"Make your time count."

TALK

As I shuffle down the crowded hallway
after school, my mind still spins
the same question:

Did Zoe do it on purpose?

She passes right by me,
a cold wind scraping my cheek.

Determined to get an answer
I turn and follow her.
"We need to talk,"
I say over her shoulder.

Zoe opens her locker,
shoves her books onto the shelf.
      "Oh, yeah? What changed?"

People push. Jostle me.
I struggle to stay close.
Lockers bang shut on either side of her,
kids scatter down the hall.
I step forward

but she's the one who starts talking.
        "You disappeared, Brynn. Again.
        You obviously don't care
        so, why don't you just do
        what you always do—"
she waves her hand to dismiss me,
        "...go away."

272

I DON'T

I root myself beside Zoe
but I might as well not be there
for all the talking I'm doing,
and suddenly, she's walking down the hall.
I run after.   "Wait!"
She whirls around so fast, we nearly crash.
I blink. She frowns.
>"What, Brynn?
>Do you have something to *say*
>or not?"

Her tone
triggers that old feeling
that my words never add up to enough.
Why speak at all?
The thought comes in a flash,
but it's too long for Zoe.
>"Didn't think so."

FROM BELOW

My pulse roars in my head,
and similar to the way water
bubbles up from the ground,
my emotions come to the surface.

Her back is to me, still walking away,
but the words pour out of me.

"You set me up!"

Zoe turns,
walks back slowly,
speechless.

But I have more than enough words now
to fill the gap between us.

"It was *your* idea to go to your house.
You insisted
without explaining the real reason why.
You knew the risk

"and when your mom showed up,
she blamed me—

274

thought I *convinced* you to miss that interview.
You let her rip me apart.
And it was because of what *you* did.

"I was in the wrong place
at the wrong time
because of *you*.

"So, tell me, Zoe—why—*why*
was I *really* there…?"
I stick out my chin.
"Did you plan it out
or just take advantage
of the opportunity?"

STUNG

Zoe's shock is visible.
     "You're wrong—
  I didn't mean
      to set you up.
        I just…
            wanted one
          afternoon
    with someone who understands
        who I really am."
Her eyes flit from mine.
     "I thought you did."

It's what I've wanted to hear, what I've wanted
to believe

yet I feel stung.

ANGER GROWS

"Maybe I *don't*.   Understand
who you really are.   Do you
understand who I am?   Maybe not.

"Because if you did, you'd know
that the things your mom said
burned a hole right through me

"And the fact that we did what we did
and you led me to believe you wanted more
than to just mess around

"But you didn't even try to defend me
as if I was
exactly what your mom said—
nothing but a waste of your time

"And even later, you didn't apologize.
You only complained
about your phone and computer
being taken away

"Never mind how I felt
or what had happened to me.

"You never asked,
so you didn't know that I ended up
getting caught in that blizzard

"because I was so torn up,
I wasn't thinking,
so I kept running

"And it was bad,
but I'll spare you the details

"because that's just me, right?
I *roam about   going nowhere*."

Zoe shakes her head,
and her mouth opens to speak.

"No.   You *listen*.
Zoe, you complain about your mom,
and I know it's not easy. I know. But Zoe—

"At least you have your mom.   You have
a chance to show her   who you really are.

"Don't waste it!"

278

SAME BUT DIFFERENT

I run.
Not to escape her words.
But to leave mine behind.

BREATHLESS

I gasp for breath in the middle of the school lawn,
and it dawns on me that not only have I left
all my things in my locker,
but also,
Miss Cooper expects me in the art room.

Zoe catches up but stands behind me.
        "You're right."
I turn around.
        "I shouldn't have put you
        in that position."
Wind tosses her hair around her face,
curls loose and free.
She visibly shivers, but I can't tell
if it's because she's only wearing a thin t-shirt
or if it's her emotions.
        "My mom was horrible to you.
        I didn't mean
        for things to turn out the way they did.
        But they did.
        And I'm sorry.   I really am.
        And I *did* tell her
        that it *wasn't* your fault.
        She no longer blames you.

But you're right—
I should've asked about you—
stopped to think about what you
were going through."
The look in her eyes pleads with me.

I don't know how to answer.

Her hands ball into fists.
        "Meeting you—being with you—
changed how I see myself.
I've got to sort that out on my own.
I know that.
But it would be nice to have someone
to talk with, be with.
Know what I mean?"

My focus bounces between the intensity
in her eyes, the golden glints shining,
and the freckles across her cheekbones,
that remind me of shadows in dappled light.

        "I've been here all year, Brynn,
and you keep disappearing.
I know I screwed up.
But it's more than just you and me.

"Maybe my mom is right
about one thing—
she doesn't want me to get dragged down.

"I've been watching you fall all year.
I can't keep hanging on, hoping…."

I step back.
She is quick to catch my sleeve, pull me close.
        "Hey, I know you lost your mom.
        You have every right
        to be angry,
        sad,
        and everywhere in between.
        But stop running.
        Ask for help if you need it.
        Let *somebody* in."

INTERUPTED

The sound of Kim's car horn
cuts between us
Zoe leaves me standing alone
watching her run

FIRST INSTINCT

I wish I could fold up,
tuck myself inside of an old, hollow oak tree
Break down into soil
Decompose

INSTEAD, I GO TO THE ART ROOM

Miss Cooper looks up
when I walk through the door.
        "Didn't think you were coming."
My bag thuds to the floor. "Sorry."
I start picking up chairs,
set them on the tables upside down,
feel Miss Cooper's gaze on my back.
        "Everything okay?"
I blink away tears, croak, "Fine,"
pass through the archway to the ceramics room.
I want to get my hands dirty.
Build something.
But spinning the wheel gets me nowhere.
My hands can't grasp or let go.
Can't shape, let alone center.

NOT YOUR ENEMY

"Can I just ask…?"
Miss Cooper waits for me to glance up.
She's across the room,
leaning against the doorframe.
"What did that clay do to you?"
I take my hands off the messy lump. "Huh?"
Her eyes twinkle.
"You look like you're trying to
strangle it."
Her laugh is light
as she walks around the worktables.
"Remember, you can't control it.
And it won't move
until you move."
She sits at the wheel beside mine
no clay in her hands.
She holds her body rigid, tense. Then loose.
"See the difference?"
I slump, not relaxed,
just discouraged. Even this
I can't get right.
Her voice is gentle.
"Remember to work *with* the clay.
It's not your enemy."

I nod, blinking away new tears.

Her forehead furrows. Her voice softens.

    "You know, if you need to talk,

    I'm here."

I shake my head and try to smile.

If I try to speak, I'm afraid I'll only cry.

After a long moment, she checks the clock.

    "Well, it's time to clean up.

    You can try again tomorrow."

I start scraping the clay from the wheel.

Before she goes back into the other room,

Miss Cooper says,

    "I know you can do this, Brynn.

    Trust yourself."

ON MY WALK

Moody gray skies
       turn to drizzle,
       then rain

Water
       carves channels from the ridgetop
       to the creek,
       seeps through cracks in my shoes

I struggle to climb

Shoelace
       snags on a tree root

My foot
       slips

             I

                   fall

RAW

Broke open

I am a wild beast
letting out loud, ugly sobs,
hot tears mixing with cool rain

Panting hard
I am washed clean

DOWN

Cheek-to-cheek with mud
I smell wet leaves
earth
decay

I roll onto my back

squeeze my eyes shut,
let myself soak in the sound—
cold splashes on my face:
thup-thup-thup-thup

LAYERS

Zoe is right—I *have* been falling
like rainwater down these hills,
rushing to the bottom.

Water always flows to the lowest point.

Mom is never coming back. This truth comes
day after day, remembering it
layer after layer after layer
for who knows how long.

Mom is never coming back. Yet, life goes on.

thup-thup-thup-thup

SILENCE AND SOUND

It's not her death, but my life
Green growing through ash

THROUGH THE DOWNPOUR

Running back to town
Raindrops pummeling my skin
Each one asking   *How?*

RUGGED MOUNTAIN & CO.

I duck into the first dry spot on my route home,
a specialty store
known for outdoor clothing,
high-tech camping gear.
I wipe my shoes on the floor mat, glance up.
The cashier and customer at the register
frown at me.
To my horror, the cashier
is Nina. My former best friend.
She blurts:
  "What happened to you?"
When I don't answer,
she points to the back.
  "Bathroom's that way."
Her look tells me I'd better clean up
or get out.
  "Umbrellas are aisle three."
She returns her attention to scanning items,
comments to the guy,
  "Hope you're not camping tonight!"
A tent and sleeping bag are on the counter.
I don't wait to hear his reply.

BOOTS

After washing up and drying off,
I wander the aisles to wait out the storm.
Find a pair of woolen socks.
A row of leather boots.
Strong and sturdy.

You need a good pair of boots.
Mom said the day before she died.

I hadn't wanted to accept the idea.

All this time I've been wrapping
and rewrapping
cracks,
determined to keep things the same.

Truth is
my feet are wet.

I wiggle out of my shoes,
strip off my socks,
put on the woolen pair,
the leather boots,
do a test walk.

IT'S A START

At the register, Nina gives me a quick once-over,
then greets me with a smile,
most likely relieved to see that I'm dry.
            "Did you find everything you need?"
A standard question, meaning store products.
It makes me pause, though.

Keeping my feet dry is one needed change, but
fixing cracks in life
will take much more than buying a new pair
of boots.

            Daniel will take you shopping….

Maybe   what Mom meant
was not about boots but, rather,
            that Daniel
would help me with the changes ahead.

I smile back at Nina. "I think so."

296

QUESTIONS AND ANSWERS

Nina looks inside the box,
notices my sopping-wet shoes.
      "Those poor things
        didn't have a chance in that rain."
Laughter rolls out of her—
a sound that triggers happy memories.
Nina tilts her head.
      "How're things?"
I brace myself. Think she's asking
because of Mom.
But she surprises me.
      "You know—with that new girl…Zoe?
      Saw you two at Compass Café
      a while back."
I hadn't noticed Nina.
Didn't expect her to notice me and Zoe.
Didn't even know I still showed up on her radar.
My cheeks flush.
She punches a key on the register.
      "You looked happy."
I wonder if she's making fun of me.
But no one is here to watch. She sounds
like her old self.
I decide to trust.

Wish I could report that Zoe and I are still
happy,
but I'm far from certain about anything
involving Zoe.
I simply smile.
And, although Nina is being kind,
I'm under no illusion
that she'll start being my friend again.
She tells me my total, and I pay with cash.
Money from my first paycheck.
I might still have more questions than answers,
but, for now, it's enough
to share a smile with an old friend.

PORCH STEP

My boots make a different sound
than my shoes
running up the porch stairs,
and, again, I notice how the creaky step
is now sturdy. Quiet.
I go back down and bounce on it.
       Smile.

Those yew stumps still stick up awkwardly,
and I can't help but frown.

It's time
to finish letting them go—
come up with a plan.
One that Mom would be proud of.

During dinner, I ask Daniel
for help.

We decide to let time   and microbes
turn those stumps into soil.   We'll cut
their trunks to below ground level,
cut their roots, then backfill with dirt,
let the change   happen slowly.

Over bowls of ice cream, we sit side by side,
selecting plants from the catalogue,
      imagining the garden that Mom
         talked about planting,
then draw a design.

All the while, in the back of my mind,
the question stirs:
what do *I* want next in life?

DIGGING

Monday after school
in front of our house,
spade in hand

I cut through sod, dig into earth,
lift it up and out.
Dig deeper.
Spill the dirt into a pile.

Breathe in the scent of opened soil.

The movements of my body give my mind
time to turn over
what I want.
What I've always wanted.

To return to the farm.

I will not let go so easily.

HABIT

Around each yew,
trenches reach three feet deep
by three feet wide.

Daniel cuts the stumps with a chainsaw.
I sever feeder roots with a pruning saw.

A musky scent fills the air.

We stand back, take stock
of our work, drink from our water bottles,
catch our breath.

When Daniel asks me what's on my mind,
instead of shrugging off the question
like my usual habit,
I start talking.

OPENING UP

Our conversation turns toward Mom
the way the creek curves,
like it was always meant to.

I scoop soil from the pile,
backfill one of the trenches.

"Do you think Mom knew
she was dying?"

Daniel works beside me,
scooping and filling.
He pauses.
      "I don't know."

"Did you and she ever talk
about what might happen if she did…?"

He leans on the wooden handle of his shovel.
      "During that first hospital stay,
      your mom said she didn't want
      to be one of those patients who
      walk around with Death
      always on her shoulder.

I promised to help her."
He scoops more soil.
"We mostly talked about you.
Stories about when you were young.
How much she enjoyed
being your mom.
Since then, I've wondered, though."
He stops.
"The only future she discussed
was yours."

GOODBYE

If the only future Mom discussed was mine,
why didn't she talk about it with me?

I continue to spread out soil,
fill in the empty spaces, but I'm tempted to run,
leave all my feelings behind me.

Instead, I stop shoveling,
stop moving.

I speak up.

"How could Mom write her last will,
ask me to decide about her ashes
but never
talk about dying?
You all kept saying
she was going to get *better*.
Why did you let me rely
on that hope?
Why didn't you make me *see*?"

Daniel's eyes pool with sadness.
    "I'm sorry, Brynn.

We *all* hoped. We really thought…."
He shakes his head, his voice tight with tears.
        "Honestly, I don't think
        your mother knew how
        to talk about it.
        She *wanted* to be here.
        Didn't want to miss a single thing."
I blink away my own tears.
        "She did what she could, Brynn.
        She focused her time on *living*.
        Try to remember, she was never good
        at goodbyes."

SEE YOU LATER

Realization swoops in like a barn swallow.
Of course.

Mom focused on *next time*.
Never said goodbye.
It was always and only—
      I whisper:
          "See you later."
Daniel nods.

Even if Mom did know,
she was never going to say *goodbye*.

UP IN MY BEDROOM

I turn to what I know—
I open that big bin of magazines Mom saved,
and the box of old photographs
from the basement,
start sorting, cutting
connecting
my past to my future.
Make decisions
about placement of words and pictures,
put the pieces into envelopes,
this time, certain
about where they're going.

TAKING SHAPE

My hands shape clay, moving ever forward,
toward completing a bowl on the wheel for the
Art Show. Moving forward   by staying steady,
moving slowly from the bottom, up, in circles,
allowing myself to move with   the clay.
Responding with kindness to what I
notice.   In me   and in the clay.
I listen and converse.

A FAVOR

"I have to go somewhere,"
I tell Zoe before first bell,
"…and I haven't wanted to go."
I shove my hands into my pockets.
Inhale a shaky breath before explaining.
"Not since my mom died."

She waits.

"It's the little cemetery north of town.
It's where my family's plot is—"
She nods, and I ask,
"Will you go with me?"

Her face brightens,
and her tone makes it sound as though
instead of asking for a favor,
I've given her a gift.
       "Of course."

NORTH OAK CEMETERY

The oak trees that grace the cemetery
greet us like old friends, their budding leaves
a sign of summer dancing ever closer,
taking hold.

Grandpa, walking with a stiff gait, leads us in.
        "Just think, even those towering trees
        used to be small saplings
        once upon a time."
It's what he says at the beginning of every
visit to the graves.
I nod out of habit,   glance at Zoe,
catch her smile.

Before Grandpa can get into full-on
storytelling mode,
Grandma steers him away,
toward the stones marking old friends of theirs,
leaving me
to lead Zoe

to my ancestors.

MY ANCESTORS

We stand in front of the biggest stone
with BAILEY in all capital letters.

I crouch next to a smaller one,
reach my hand out,
trace the grooves of carved-out letters:
      MOTHER
I read the name—*Elizabeth*—
my great-great-grandmother.

Pale pink and white petals of shooting stars
light up the green foliage beside the gravestones.

Some of the country's last traces
of remnant prairie
grow in this cemetery, a small patch of land
with nearly 400 native plants
due to the township's agreement to not mow,
except for a few main paths.

The roots of these plants
are older
than any of the people buried here.

CONFESSION

I sit cross-legged across from Zoe
in the short grass of a path
winding under one of the oak trees.
"My grandparents want to bury
my mom's ashes here,"
I tell her, nodding toward the gravestones.
"I didn't want
to allow it," I confess, my fingers picking
at the grass.
"Not because it's a bad idea
but because it would mean
it would be done."

HOLDING ON

Zoe's eyes hold mine
until I shrug and look away.
"I also
don't want to simply agree
to make it easy. Just because they
want it.
I should choose what my mom
would want,
right?"

Zoe tilts her head to the side, considering.
> "Don't you think the point
> of her giving you this choice
> was so that you could choose
> somewhere that helps you?"

The idea never occurred to me.
She smiles.
> "Funerals are for the living, Brynn.
> They give us the opportunity
> to say our goodbyes. To remember."

"That's just it—" my voice trembles. "I never got
to say goodbye."

I recall those days leading up to Mom's death
trying to stay so still and quiet,
barely speaking a word,
not wanting to detract
from getting her well again.
Still hoping.

"I thought if I didn't take up too much space
or be too loud,
we'd get past it."
I rub the seed-laden grass between my fingers.
"I never guessed the other side
would look like this."

A red-winged blackbird calls *conk-la-reee*,
the sound that always makes me feel as though
summer is finally here
and could stretch on forever.

"Time is so strange," I say, "Mom's death
was drawn out
when I count all the months that she was sick,
but so sudden at the end,
I couldn't even be there."

My chest grows heavy,
like a boulder sinking into mud.

Zoe reaches for my hand.
I hold on.
Let my tears fall.

REMEMBERING REGRET

My voice is but a shaky whisper:
"I should've prepared myself."

Zoe squeezes my hand.
      "No, Brynn. There's no way
      to prepare for losing someone you love.
      Any more than just being there
      loving all you can
      while you can.
      Even then…."
She allows time for my tears. Then softly says,
      "…Brynn, it's *always* a shock.
      You can't help but hope
      a little bit longer.
      And when someone's been sick
      for a long time, like your mom,
      you never know *when.*
      That weight of not knowing
      is hard to keep holding.
      But even that kind of death feels sudden
      because they're here
      until they're not,"
her voice drifts,
      "…that's how it was with my grandfather

…Pop-Pop."
She looks long and hard at the budding canopy.
        "And Nana will be the same—"
Her voice trips over emotion. Her eyes close.

Her nana,
I remember,
        who used to put cinnamon
        in hot chocolate.

I blink the tears from my eyelashes,
look at her closely,
ask, "What do you mean?
What about your nana?"

GETTING CLOSER

In a stream of words, I see colors in Zoe
I've never noticed before—
a past I haven't asked about. Too wrapped up
in my own troubles. Now I hear
that her nana

          is the reason
          Zoe and her mom moved
          to small-town life in Prairie Hill.

Her nana, who for years

          offered Zoe freedom
          from her mother's strict rules
          during summers and holidays,
          had always given her strength
          and support,

now stayed in assisted living   because

      "After Pop-Pop died, it wasn't safe.
      She's a danger to herself and others.
      Nana's even forgetting…me."

I realize Zoe knows grief
so big,
so terrible,
so much like mine, yet
different.

Instead of getting swallowed by it,
her eyes open.
  "Change
  is hard enough to understand, but death
  is final. Our minds…."
She shakes her head.
  "It feels impossible to comprehend.
  It's always too soon."

"So, what do we do?"
My question feels so large,
it seems only the trees,
hills, or sky
could possibly answer

but Zoe's voice blooms softly,
  "Keep on loving?"

I breathe it in slowly.
"Yes."

I squeeze her hand.

Keep on loving.

PIECES COME TOGETHER

With the envelopes spilled out across the table,
I set to work, putting my design into place—
words begin to circle my newly fired bowl:

She called me   Stardust.   Taught me to dip my toes
into the cold creek   Touch   the down of milkweed,
set their seeds free.   Everyone   every   person   is a wild
flower.   A mighty oak.   Let us   set down our own
roots.   Allow ourselves   and each other   space
to s t r e t c h   w i d e   dig deep.
Find our own direction, what's most
important   to   us.

I brush mod-podge over
letter after letter, over
photos of mom and me. Of the land
we loved together.

When I'm finished, I text a message—
call a family meeting.

WITH EACH STEP, TRUTH SINKS IN

Mom's dream
     took root in the house and garden,
     working among books,
     and our family of three

while mine
     is entwined with the farm.

I know that Mom is not
in those back woods   but
my memory of her is strong there,
and not only that—
I feel my future   waiting

wanting to engage with the land
based on the principles of permaculture,
grounded by old roots
and seeking balance
by working with
change

because I now see
that we can never go back
to the way things were before.

Before Mom died. Or, for that matter
any other point
in our ecological history.

It's about moving forward,
moving toward
deeper connection.

A VISION

Daniel and I talk late into the night,
exploring every option, angle, and alternative—
Different ways to find a solution,
until we draw up—not just a plan—
but a vision.

DECISION

At the old farmhouse
Grandpa sits beside Grandma on the couch,
Daniel in the rocking chair.

Grandma's fingers move fast
with needle and thread
connecting a square of blue velvet
to a square of faded denim—
remnants
of Mom's old clothes left in our basement.

The other day, I handed the pile over.
Told Grandma,
she would know what to do.

She's sewing a memory quilt.

I stand, ready to speak.
Clear my throat.
Grandma's fingers slow. She looks up.

One breath in, then,
"I've decided what I'd like to do."

TELLING THEM

My words rush like feet
stepping across stones.

"I know it's important to you
to have a place to go to honor Mom,
and that our family plot
has always been where you wanted her to be.
…I want to honor that."

Grandma and Grandpa share a glance.

"Mom used to tell me that our family
mingled
with the roots of the original prairie.
She seemed to love that idea,
and so do I.
So…"

I take a deep breath,
make it final.
"…we'll bury some of her ashes there,"

my heart beats faster,
"…but not all."

326

ANOTHER WAY

My grandparents exchange confused expressions.
I blaze on.
"I also know that you want to help us
by selling the farm.
That you don't want us to lose our house.
That you're getting older
and the farm is hard to manage.
And that someone has already made you an offer.
But Daniel and I have talked…."
I glance at him, afraid he's changed his mind,
but he nods for me to go on. I stand taller.
"We believe there's another way."

WHAT COLLAGE HAS TAUGHT ME

Sometimes the answer reveals itself
through the process of
rearranging
realigning.

It's about noticing the relationships between
all parts. Finding
the best place for each piece
to thrive.

As I explain our ideas,
Grandma and Grandpa lean forward.
Listen closely.

The four of us spend the rest of the evening
in discussion,
making lists and sorting details.

ONE AND ONLY

Before we leave for the night,
Grandma rests a hand on my back,
leans close.
    "Thank you.
    For honoring our wishes.

    "Your mother was our daughter.
    Our one and only.
    Our focus for so long."
She rubs my back and smiles.
    "But she's left us *her*
    one and only,
    and it's time to focus on what *you* need.

    "Thank you for telling us, my dear."

MOM'S POCKET PRAIRIE

"Did I hear you ordered some plants?"
Grandpa calls through the open truck window
as he pulls into our driveway.
Dana and I laugh, rising from the porch step.

Frank rolls up on his bike.
"Just in time!"
Dana and Frank have already spent
the last couple of days with me,
digging up more sod
and prepping soil.

Grandma brings in a grocery bag and her stew pot
while we unload the plant trays.

Grandpa leaves the planting to us three,
telling us to enjoy our days of limber knees,
and as we work, we joke around and talk about
plans for the summer
until we're finally out of plants to plant,
and the only thing to do
is clean up.

Daniel gets home from work just as Grandma

comes out to ask,
        "You all hungry?"
When she sees the garden, she gasps,
then calls through the screen door,
        "Hank, get out here!"

Grandpa does, and we all stand back,
looking at the design we've made.
Bunches of little blue stem and prairie dropseed
fill in between
purple coneflower, butterfly weed
anise hyssop, wild bergamot,
orange coneflower, and smooth blue aster.

Grandma's voice cracks,
        "Your mother would love it."

It's a beginning—the plants are still small—
but Daniel smiles at us
        as though he's seeing
        what it will become.

        "You did it."

AROUND THE TABLE

Dana walks into the kitchen, tries to
peek into the stew pot.
        "Mmm-mmm. Smells delicious!"
Frank sees the rhubarb pie on the counter.
        "Can we eat dessert first?"
Grandma laughs,
sets a basket of bread on the table.
        "No, but the first person to wash up
        and sit down will get the first slice."
After washing their hands, Frank and Dana
race to the table. Dana wins,
but Frank just laughs. He turns to Daniel.
        "Did you really
        play in a jazz band in Chicago?"
Daniel's eyes twinkle
as he tells of his college days,
including some stories that I've never heard.

A smile drifts over my lips.

Mom's garden was one step in the plan.
There's still more to do, but for now,
glancing around the table
I feast on joy.

ONE DAY AWAY

In class, Miss Cooper reminds us
          we all have something to say.
Deep meaning is implied, but

Dana mumbles under her breath:
      "Fancy way of saying
      talk for three minutes straight."

Miss Cooper doesn't hear.
She says the Art Show is our chance
    to be bold.

ACORN

The library is packed with people.
Miss Cooper must be happy that art
is getting so much support from our small town
but my throat begins to tighten.

I reach into my trouser pocket,
finger the edges of folded paper.
Try to taste the words
I wrote down last night.

In my other pocket, I find an acorn.
Hope it brings
what my grandfather claims:
good luck.

DANA PRESENTS

Dana rushes through a ramble,
admitting to the crowd that she never liked
getting her hands dirty, but
now she doesn't mind so much.
She didn't really like
any of the pots she made,
but if taking Ceramics could be boiled down
to just one word,
she says it would be *persistence*
and that's something worthwhile.

RAINBOW WOMAN

Zoe's voice draws me
closer. I peer between shoulders
watch her.

Her painting is of a young woman
grounded in space
still and quiet, yet moving with colors

combining
contrasting
moving beyond

BELLA

I don't know what makes me glance over,
but perhaps it is the orange dress
that catches my eye,
or the white curls
that bob along with everything Zoe is saying.
I can only see the woman's profile,
but immediately I realize she is Bella
from the art studio next to Compass Café.
My own smile grows
because seeing her
reminds me that Zoe has truly
painted her dream come true.
This summer
she won't be making house flyers on a computer.
She'll be
putting her artistic eye to good use
because she'll be
working at Bella's studio.

INSIDE

Inside the rigid box designed for her.
The one her mother thinks will keep
Zoe safe.   That girl, with paintbrush,
is finding each crack between the seams
where her roots
                 can slip through,
                          cause the joints
                                      to snap.

NO GETTING AROUND IT

When it's my turn…just as I predicted,
it isn't my pottery so much as my grief

on display.

It's not that people are whispering gossip.
I choose to go there.

"As many of you know…"

I stop to wonder which word or phrase to use,
but there's no sugarcoating. No getting around it.

No denying.

I say it like it is:
"…my mom died."

OUT LOUD

Saying it out loud to so many people, all at once,
kicks my adrenaline into overdrive,
causing my whole body to shake

but I know I must walk across this wide-open
silence.

I must connect
what I've just said
to something next.

"Working with clay on the wheel,"
I indicate the finished bowl in my hands,
"…has helped me."

I gulp in air, trying to recall the notes
folded inside my pocket.

Then, despite the many possible choices,
my focus locks on the one set of eyes
I'd rather not meet:

Kim's.

NOISE

Kim is standing in the back.
She's not speaking—
no one is.   But noise
creeps in like flames burning thatch.

What she said before:
You're nothing….

threatens to fold me into ash.

I wonder if her words are all
that I am.

THE WHOLE PICTURE

My own two hands
are what save me—
my fingers that feel the texture
of all the pieces
that make up the whole picture
circling my bowl.

These hands—after practicing with clay—
now know what it feels like to work *with*
resistance,
instead of fight it.
Let go
as well as hold on.

These fingers that dipped down into cool mud
last summer, holding a heart
full of questions.

At last, I feel as though some answers
are within my grasp:

Kim was wrong.

Just because I'm a quiet person

doesn't make other people's words about me
automatically valid.

Even if they're louder.

I may be a quiet person,
but I also have things to say.

It will take time and practice
before these truths
fully sink in,
like learning to work with clay
and grieving my mom's death.

I will pull these truths
into my being
just as prairie roots pull rainwater
deep into the soil,
drinking up nutrients,
so the plants can grow.

Now, gauging the expectant crowd,
I breathe in.
Let my quiet way
carve out space
for me to fill.

Remind myself
to begin again.

I dig my roots deep,
lift my voice,
sprout new life.

BACK

Afterwards, most of the crowd moves on,
but Daniel and my grandparents
stay
and Maggie, the assistant librarian,
stays, too.
She smiles wide, shaking her head.
      "Gosh, weren't you that little kid
      with scraped knees
      running up and down our aisles
      just a day or two ago?"
She lets out a hearty laugh.
      "Don't be a stranger, okay?"
There's no room for pity in her eyes.
Only love.
It feels good to be back.

LATER, IN MY FAVORITE CORNER

I find Zoe sitting in the same chair,
head down,
drawing in a sketchbook.

I point to the chair across from hers.
"This seat taken?"

WHEN I SEE IT

I have no clue how it got there,
but displayed on top of a low bookshelf
behind Zoe,
is the decoupage log.

Mr. Lewis kept asking me to take it home,
but like so much in my life, I put it off.

A small sign reads:
>*Donated in Memory of Lori Bailey*
>*Created by Brynn Bailey and Zoe McClain*

Zoe blushes.
>"It felt like the right thing to do."

It's as if a piece to a puzzle
clicks into place. "Perfect."

SPRING BLOSSOMS INTO SUMMER

BECAUSE

Because I both listened and spoke up
and because the people in my life did the same

our lives are taking shape.

The Prairie-Craftsman has been sold
to a young family who love
        the new garden.

My grandparents sold only half
        of the farm, leaving the other
half for Daniel and me.

Profits from those two sales
paid off the medical debt.

Now, Daniel and I live in the old farmhouse.
We pay rent to my grandparents,
so they can pay rent in town
for a cute apartment
one block south of Compass Café.

Day by day, I'm moving forward
toward making my vision come true.

A farm about balance.
Good for nature
people
and the future.

Just like working with clay,
my life takes shape
every time I decide
when to let go and when to hold on.

PLACES TO REST

We gather in August
the chorus of insects singing in the heat
red-winged black birds aloft compass plants
oak branches stretching wide.

We lay Mom's ashes to rest

in the family plot next to a stone with her name—
        where our ancestors
        mingle with prairie roots,
in the restored prairie, along the trail—
        where she and Daniel worked
        and fell in love
in the back woods
        where the child I was
        meets the woman I'll become.

THIS DECISION

Whether she knew it or not,
this decision was Mom's last gift to me—
a chance to choose.

To listen to myself
and embrace who I am.

Seeing that, for me,
it's in those quiet outdoor spaces
where love

walks across silence.

PERSEIDS AGAIN, BUT THIS TIME

Zoe's hand fits into mine
walking past the four oak trees.

Twilight settles over the farm,
and I carry a blanket because we plan to stay
long after the air cools.

We've come to see the falling stars,
but right now, I watch points of light rising.
Thousands of fireflies
connecting in the night.

Zoe leans against my shoulder.
  "You gonna make a wish?"

I squeeze her hand.
"Don't need to."

Acknowledgements

Writing is both a quiet endeavor and a cause for much noise in one's head. Without the many people who took the time to listen and talk with me, this book wouldn't have been published.

A huge thank you goes to my critique groups and early readers. To Ingrid Kallick, Zach Elliot, Sue Brewster, Tom McKay, Ben Doran, and Renee Ryan, thank you for your time and thoughtful feedback; nothing was too great or too small to be considered carefully. To Ellie Schatz, who saw my earliest drafts, thank you for believing in me. And to Hillarie Kane, thank you for your unwavering confidence in this story.

Special thanks to Kathi Appelt, for your advice and encouragement at just the right moment.

Thank you to the Society of Children's Book Writers & Illustrators (SCBWI), especially Bridget Birdsall, who, as my SCBWI-WI mentor in 2019, challenged me to take an even closer look at my manuscript and dig deeper.

Thanks to OutReach in Madison, WI, and all the kind people I met there long ago. Thanks for helping me to feel seen.

The kernel of Brynn and Zoe's story was born during my time working at the University of Wisconsin-Platteville Writing Center. Thank you, first, to Dr. Andrea Cool, and then, to Evelyn Martens, for the many in-depth conversations about finding balance between talking and listening within the context of tutoring to help writers develop their own voices. Thank you to Dr. Debbie Kinder for handing me the first verse novel I ever read and for assigning the project that got me writing the beginnings of this story.

Thank you to Susan Cain for writing the book, *Quiet*, which proved that the world needs quiet people, too, and that quiet can be strong.

This writing journey has lasted years, and I couldn't have done it without the wisdom and compassion from these amazing women: Abby Mensing, Melissa Harris, Tania Richley, Mona Cassis, and Morgan Hood.

To all my parents, thank you for always loving me and for sharing with me your love of books.

Love and thanks to Nick, for those first hugs by my locker and for every cherished moment since. And to Lu, for being your ever-evolving, wonderful self.

To all the beauty in the world, and to all those who see it. Thank you for being here.

And to you, dear reader, thank you. Stretch wide and dig deep.

About the Author

Kate McKinney is a writer, mother, gardener, and sometimes trombone player. She lives in the Driftless Area of Wisconsin with her family, each year digging her roots deeper into the soil. *When to Hold On* is her debut novel.

9 781736 539019